# WAKINGS, WOOINGS, AND WRONGDOINGS

PADDY'S PEELERS MYSTERY

BOOK FIVE

AUBREY WYNNE

Editing by The Editing Hall

❀ Formatted with Vellum

# SERIES LIST

Keep updated on future releases, exclusive excerpts, and prizes by following my newsletter:

https://www.subscribepage.com/k3f1z5

**Once Upon a Widow series (sweet Regency)**

Earl of Sunderland #1
A Wicked Earl's Widow #2
Rhapsody and Rebellion #3
Earl of Darby #4
Earl of Brecken #5
Earl of Griffith #6
Beware a Wallflower's Wrath #7
A Wallflower's Wassail Punch #8
The Scoundrel's Christmas Challenge #9
The Duplicate Duke #10
Merry Mazes and Mistletoe Magic #11
Kiss the Scoundrel Farewell #12

**A Paddy's Peelers Mystery series**

Crime, Conspiracies, and Courtship #1

Pads, Purses, and Plum Pudding #2

Poisons, Potions, and Parasols #3

Rogues, Rotters, and Rubies #4

Wakings, Wooings, and Wrongdoings #5

**Read on Kindle Unlimited**

**A MacNaughton Castle Romance (steamy Regency Highland series)**

A Merry MacNaughton Mishap (Prequel) (only sweet romance in series)

Deception and Desire #1

Allusive Love #2

A Bonny Pretender #3

# WAKINGS, WOOINGS, AND WRONGDOINGS

**By**

**Aubrey Wynne**

# INTRODUCTION

The *Oxford English Dictionary,* defines *underworld* as: 1. Sublunary or terrestrial world. 4.a. A shere or region lying or considered to lie below the ordinary one. Hence also (figurative) a lower, or the lowest, stratum of society 4.b. The world of criminal or of organized crime (usually with *the*); hence, the inhabitants of this region.

***This was the world of Paddy's Peelers.***

"For alongside the world of *Pride and Prejudice* and the Nature poets there existed a pulsating, undisciplined urban underworld of young thieves, body-snatchers and gamblers. Pleasure-seekers and criminals alike were enjoying a final fling before the coming of the Metropolitan Police in 1829. Gambling and drinking were endemic in upper- and lower-class society, fraud in the middle classes."

Donald A Low *The Regency underworld*

# PADDY'S STORY

## *The Story of Paddy's Peelers*

peeler, *n.* 1816

...Originally: a member of the Irish constabulary. Later: (more *gen.*) a police officer; *spec.* a member of the original London Metropolitan force...

Patrick O'Brien, previously of the Dublin Police Force, left Ireland with his wife Margaret and arrived in London in 1798. Paddy was frustrated with the lack of government involvement in crime and the poor, unreliable pay received by officers. He wanted to belong to an organized body of policing.

Margaret's stepbrother worked as a Bow Street Runner, and this new policing force greatly interested O'Brien. It was directly attached to the magistrates and court housed at 4 Bow Street and received some funds from the central government through grants. The Runners were to become the model of the future, proving to the government and the public that a professional police force could reduce crime.

O'Brien soon gained a reputation at the Bow Street court for his clever and expedient investigations. While his professional life provided him great satisfaction, his personal life was lacking. Paddy and his wife lamented the absence of children in their household.

When Paddy stumbled across a sick waif in an alley of Whitehall, he brought the lad home. Over the next ten years, their "family" grew to a brood of seven. The couple developed the unique talents of their six boys and one girl. As the children grew into adulthood, O'Brien created a detective agency that utilized the skills of his brood. All the men spent an allotted time as a constable for Bow Street, learning the trade from seasoned runners while working in the "family business."

Nicknamed Paddy's Peelers (*peeler* slang for an Irish policeman), O'Brien's crew became an efficient team that included detectives, a physician that doubled as a coroner for autopsies, a solicitor who specialized in criminal law, a female master of disguise able to infiltrate any level of society, and a barrister who later joined their ranks to present certain cases pro bono in High Court.

# PROLOGUE

*February 1800*
*Cheapside, London*

Benjamin shuffled along next to the silent man. An icy puddle loomed before them, and he quickly sidestepped it so the cold, mucky water wouldn't seep into his shoes. But he swerved too wide and ran into Smitty.

"Watch yerself, boy," said Smitty with a slap to Ben's head.

Benjamin rubbed the back of his head with his good arm, wiping the snowflakes from his neck. His right elbow was twice the size it should be, and it hurt worse than the switch they'd used on him at the workhouse.

Three months ago, he'd watched as the stranger handed some coins to the mistress and was ordered to go with the man, leaving the only home he'd ever known. Benjamin had thought his life was improving. He'd been told he would be *an apprentice,* which sounded very important.

*"Whatcha gonna use him for?" asked Mrs. Benson. "Apprentice for what?"*

*"What's it to ye?" asked the man with a sneer. "Ye wantin' more blunt?"*

*She shook her head. "Just don't tell anyone where ye got him, then."*

At first, Benjamin hadn't minded crawling up the narrow chimneys, cleaning the flues, and sliding down. It was warm inside the narrow, cramped ducts as he pushed his brush up ahead of his body and cleared the soot. The dust got in his eyes, and they seemed to be constantly swollen. Smitty said it was Ben's own fault because he rubbed them. The soot also coated his throat, giving him a chronic cough.

He didn't get much to eat, but it was more than what he'd been fed at the workhouse. Smitty wanted him healthy but small, or Ben would get too big to do the work.

"Then I'll have to put ye in a sack and toss ye in the Thames," Smitty had said with a guffaw. "Like them mewling kittens the cat had last week."

Ben had decided a semi-full belly and fewer beatings were better than daily beatings and being constantly hungry. He could take his mind off hunger pains, unlike the sores and bruises. Plus, he had his own corner in the kitchen by the hearth. Since it was his job to start the fire each morning for the cook, he often woke cold and was able to stoke the embers.

But a few days ago, they'd gone to a four-story tenement with seven flues. The longer flues of the bottom floor were connected at awkward angles, and Ben had found himself stuck more than once. On the last one, his foot had hit a loose brick on the way down. He slipped, scraping his arms and back against the rough, hot surface. To his horror, his knees were soon bent beneath his chin, and he was stuck.

Ben had heard of boys dying in the flues, with men having to remove bricks to retrieve their bodies. With that image in his head, he frantically pushed his forearms against the tight enclosure, wiggling and pulling and pushing until he was able to stretch his legs again. He heard the material rip at the knees of his trousers, felt the burn from the heavy scrapings. Smitty would be angry, for he'd have to buy him another pair. But the real pain came from his arm. He'd smacked his elbow hard during the struggle. Tears streaked his blackened cheeks when he'd emerged from the chimney, and Smitty had threatened to give him something worthy of those tears.

So as Ben looked up at the three-story building in front of them, a tavern with living quarters above, he prayed this job would be a quick one. Every foot up would be severe and awful. Holding his aching joint, Ben followed Smitty into a large, shadowy room. The windows were filthy, limiting the amount of winter light needed to brighten the interior.

As his eyes grew accustomed to the dark surroundings, he saw several men on one side of the room. The barkeep stood behind a long plank serving as a counter. "Got a new boy, eh?" asked the burly bald man.

"Aye, he's a good 'un. Nice and skinny. Nuttin' he can't fit into," said Smitty with a pleased smile, squeezing Benjamin's shoulder with an extra hard pinch of bony knuckles.

"Ye want a bumper while the lad's workin'?"

"Do ye always ask dull questions?" barked Smitty with a laugh, turning to Ben. "Now get off that coat and ready yerself."

Benjamin had stripped off his worn, dirty coat and homespun shirt when a shadow fell over them. He looked up to see a giant of a man standing in the doorway. The stranger's face was shadowed, but Ben could see the bright blue of his eyes as he removed his tall hat, revealing dark-red hair.

"G'day, gentlemen," said the newcomer, moving into the room. "Just finished a piece of work around da corner, and I'm t'irstier than a lost man in da desert."

"Afternoon, O'Brien," said the barkeep. "Whiskey?"

"Only if it's Irish, otherwise an ale," said O'Brien as he tossed a coin on the plank, his eyes landing on Benjamin. "Plannin' on taking a bath, boyo?"

Ben's eyes grew wide as O'Brien concentrated his penetrating gaze on him. Ben shook his head. "No, sir."

"Den put yer clothes on, lad. 'Tis a wee cold out there," said O'Brien, then turned back to drink the whiskey in one gulp. "Now I'll take dat ale."

"Did ye find the thief?" asked the barkeep as he set a bumper in front of the customer. "Aye, and off to Bow Street, he is."

"A thieftaker, eh?" sneered Smitty. "Make much?"

"Supports me family," said O'Brien, turning around to watch Ben again, his blue eyes narrowed. "Dat yer lad?"

Smitty nodded. "Haven't had him long. Got him fer my apprentice."

"What work would dat be?" he asked mildly as Ben picked up his brush and moved toward the hearth.

Ben reached up and felt the inner chamber and pulled back his hand, a blister already beginning on one finger. He decided to wear his shirt so as not to burn his backside. The trick was hopping up and planting his arms inside to hold his body up, so his feet wouldn't touch the glowing coals. It would be tricky with his injury.

When he returned to the chimney, he stuck his head in to judge the distance, preparing to hop into the opening.

"He's a climber," said Smitty.

"Hold up dere, boyo," said O'Brien.

When Benjamin turned to face the men, O'Brien waved him over. "How old are ye lad?"

"What do ye care how old he is?" growled Smitty. "Ain't yer boy. I'm the one who feeds and clothes the urchin."

"I wasn't askin' ye, my friend. I was askin' the boyo." The big man locked eyes with Ben. "Ye cannot be more than five."

Authority rippled off this man. The age he was supposed to say—eight years old—was forgotten as he answered the Irishman. "Maybe four, could be five." He swallowed. "Sir."

Smitty jumped to his feet, cursing. O'Brien held a palm out, stopping the man. "Don't even t'ink of hittin' the lad. Ye know as well as I da age changed to eight. And no matter what comes from the boyo's mouth, he's not as old as dat."

O'Brien stood then, towering over the other men, and approached Ben. "Let me see yer arm."

Benjamin took a step forward, but Smitty blocked him. "He ain't yer business. Benjamin, get yer coat on. We've go' other places t'go."

O'Brien planted his feet, looking down at Smitty. "I t'ink we got off on the wrong foot, so to speak," he said, his voice deep but soft. "I'm no thieftaker. I work for a magistrate, and I do have a say when the law is broken."

Smitty grabbed Ben's bad arm, and he cried out, fighting the tears. In that soft, deceptive tone, O'Brien continued, "We have t'ree choices here. Ye can leave da boyo here and go find yerself an older one. Because I'll be watchin' ye for now on. Or ye can try to leave with him, and I'll pummel ye till ye're own mother won't recognize ye. What'll it be?"

Smitty grinned, showing blackened teeth. "That's only two choices."

"Ah, ye can count! Weel, then, it seems I'm dealing with an intelligent man." O'Brien reached over and put his meaty fist around his bumper of ale and took a swallow, eyeing Smitty before setting it back down. "Yer last choice is just standin' there, and I'll give ye da same pummeling."

Smitty's mouth formed a thin line, and his hand reached under his coat. A blade glittered as he pulled it out and stepped between Benjamin and O'Brien, speaking low to Ben, "Run out the door while I take care o' this man."

Benjamin swallowed, knowing he would be punished for this encounter. He took one step, then jumped back as Smitty flew up in the air and landed on his back. The knife skittered across the filthy floor, hitting the leg of a chair and joining the echoing *crack* of Smitty's jaw.

"I had an inklin' ye'd take da second choice," O'Brien said to the unconscious man. He turned to the barkeep. "I t'ank ye for da information. Ye're a good man, Martin." O'Brien pushed a few more coins toward the business owner.

"Heard he 'ad a new boy way too young. I couldn't let it go and look Maggie in the eye," said the man, swiping the coins off the plank and into a deep pocket of his apron. "Give my best to the missus."

"Aye, and mine to yers," said O'Brien, throwing back the rest of the ale, then bending to look Benjamin in the eye, his huge hands on his equally huge thighs. "What's yer name, boyo?"

"Benjamin Cooper, sir," he said in the strongest volume he could manage. "Am I goin' back to the workhouse?"

"What do ye t'ink about a nice hot meal with a woman who'll fuss over ye and fix up dat arm of yers?"

Benjamin blinked rapidly, feeling the hot tears. He nodded, unsure if this would be a good change or not.

He'd learned not to have faith in what adults said. Unless it was bad. But something about this man told Ben he was true to his word. He would be safe. A feeling that only came when he was asleep, dreaming of the mother he didn't remember.

"Name's Paddy," said the giant. "Ye may not believe me, but in my house, we work to take care of children. Not da other way around. That don't mean ye haven't chores to do, but ye look like a lad not afraid of a bit o' hard work."

"No, sir," squeaked Ben, hating the sound of his voice. His insides were shaking, and he thought he might empty his stomach. Looking at the monstrous paw held out to him, Ben placed his small hand in the large one. The feeling was immediate as Paddy's fist closed around his. Protection, like a warm blanket that had been set near the hearth, wrapped around him. Benjamin knew, deep in his heart, he was where he was supposed to be.

Paddy led him out of the tavern, and they walked out into the cold as the sun was setting. "Consider this da first day of yer best life, boyo."

And Benjamin believed him.

# CHAPTER 1

*Cheapside, London*
*April 1821*

Benjamin Cooper hurried along the busy street, hoping his landlady still had a meal warming on the stove. It had been a long day, ending with a new and demanding client. He enjoyed his work as a solicitor, but some people could stretch a man's patience. Ahead of him, an elderly woman stumbled, her bag of produce tumbling onto the ground.

Ben and the oncoming Charley, or night watchman, both stopped to help her collect the vegetables. After a profuse and heartfelt thank-you, the woman continued on her way.

"Good evening, Mr. Felton," said Ben. "Hope you have a quiet night."

"I'll second that," said the jovial man, scratching his

jaw. His cheeks were red from the exertion of chasing rolling potatoes, and his pale-brown eyes shone from the light of the gas lamp he'd just lit. "How goes it, Mr. Cooper?"

"Business is good," said Ben. "And you?" Sam had introduced him to Mr. Felton when he'd taken Sam's rooms. He was a friendly fellow, and Ben liked him.

"Can't complain," he said. "My Kitty's started a new line of work, the opposite of my hours. So I make sure she's up when I go home, and I get a hot breakfast afore she leaves."

"Wasn't she a day maid?" asked Ben, trying to remember the man's family. Kitty must be his wife. Sam would know. He'd lived in the neighborhood much longer than Ben had at this point.

Felton nodded. "She's a knocker-up now. Says it will be a much-needed position in the future. Kitty's always been an early riser, so I think it will work out fine. Already has a half-dozen customers to wake up each morning."

Ben paused, an idea forming. "How much does she charge? I'm not an early riser, and someone ensuring I'm awake for a morning appointment would be a great boon."

"Sixpence for the week, an extra thrupence if you want her to stay until ye come to the window, and a shilling if you want her on Sunday too." He elbowed Ben in the side with a grin. "Then you get to start the day with a lovely lass smilin' at you."

"I certainly can't argue with that. Could you have her put me on the schedule?" Ben asked, amazed that a man of Felton's age still considered his wife a beauty. But then, Paddy adored Maggie, and they were in their sixth decade. Ben patted his sides to see if he had any coins on him. Today was Saturday, so he wouldn't need her until Monday. "I'll pay you now, and she can start at the beginning of next week?"

"That would be fine," said Felton. "If she can't accommodate you for some reason, I'll let you know tomorrow night when I'm on duty."

* * *

*Sunday*

*Gracechurch Street*

"That was a grand meal, Maggie, my luv," said Paddy, rubbing his belly. "No one makes a shepherd's pie like you." His faded red hair had more silver than the older man cared to admit. Not that Paddy was a vain man, but he hated that time would not stand still for him, his age slowly creeping upon his body.

Ben had seen him wince more than once as he rose from a low chair or dismounted a horse after a long ride. A smile curved Ben's mouth, remembering a young pickpocket who'd assumed Paddy O'Brien was an easy target. The youth had been kicking the air when the retired Bow Street Runner had jerked him by the collar.

"I believe you told me the same thing last month when I made one," said Nora, her green eyes flashing with mischief. She tossed a long red curl over her shoulder and pretended to pout. "Your words are like a spoonful of molasses, sweet but not quite maple syrup."

The family laughed while Paddy attempted his best martyred look.

"I ran into the neighborhood night watchman the other day," said Ben after the laughter died down. "It seems Mrs. Felton has begun her own business as a knocker-up."

"Hmm, I've heard it's getting popular with the increased industrialization in the cities," said Angus Marshall, the "family" barrister who prosecuted any cases the Peelers brought before the court. He was a brother of sorts, though not raised in the household as the original seven misfits Paddy and Maggie had collected over the years. "More people are flocking to Town for work, with no sunrise or livestock to wake them."

"My landlady used to wake me," explained Benjamin. "She's getting more and more feebleminded and often forgets. Since the girl will be knocking—or tossing something—at my window, Mrs. Blasey will never know she's forgotten."

"Let me know how that goes. I have a colleague who is always late for an early session," said Angus. He was a tall, handsome man with black hair and silver eyes. He was also an earl's by-blow. That unexpected news had sent him into a downward spiral until Paddy had found him and pulled him, literally, from the gutter. "By the way, are you interested in a new client, Ben?"

"Always," he answered, scooping the last bite of beef

and thick gravy from his plate. "I'm saving for a townhouse, then I'll begin looking for a wife."

Ben closed his eyes at the sudden cacophony of noise. Why had he said that out loud? He held his hands up. "Calm down, calm down. These are my future goals, far in the future goals. It will take years to get the funds for the property."

"I believe Paddy and I have been a good example to these children," said Maggie. Her auburn curls, streaked with gray, bounced as she nodded. "Out of the original seven, two are already married and one soon to be shackled."

Everyone turned to look at Eli, whose blue eyes now avoided his family's direct gaze. He was the youngest boy with dark-blond hair and a gentler temperament than his siblings. He had met a lovely young woman named Ruby, a cook in Hatton Garden, and they planned to marry next month. Eli's grandmother patted his hand.

"You're embarrassing my boy," Agatha Norton said with a teasing grin. "His face is almost as red as his fiancée's hair, but I agree. The fact another is contemplating the institution says ye've done something right in raisin' this brood."

"Well, let's retire to the parlor, and Nora can take over being the center of attention," said Harry, offering his hand to his wife, Lady Walters. The pair was striking with his lean, dark looks and her pale, fragile stature. "She craves it from what I understand."

"I take umbrage at that statement," Nora piped up

with a grin. "Though it's true. I took to the stage like a cat to mousing. Never regretted it."

Once in the parlor, whiskey and tea were distributed, and everyone settled into their usual spots. Aonarach, their Irish wolfhound, spread across Paddy's feet. "We'll need a bigger parlor soon," said Sam, the family physician. "Once we start having families of our own—"

"Oh, I cannot wait," interrupted Maggie. "To t'ink we were once childless..." Her dark-brown eyes misted as her gaze touched upon each face in the room. "But da good Lord had other ideas, seven of them. And now to have grandchildren to look forward to."

"See what ye've gone and done?" groused Paddy, the familiar panic in his blue eyes as he saw the tears forming in his wife's eyes. "Play a jovial tune, Nora." They all knew how much the man hated tears, whether they be happy or sad.

Nora picked up the fiddle and began a lively Irish tune while the others pushed furniture to the edge of the room. Soon, Harry and his wife, Sam and Dottie, and Clayton and Genie were dancing a reel with the O'Briens.

Ben watched his brothers and their brides twirl and hop upon the worn wool carpet. The green Wilton rug had seen better days, but no one wanted to change the room where they'd grown from homeless children to happy adults. There was the dark stain in the corner marring the otherwise gleaming hardwood floor. Clayton had tried to sneak some of Maggie's Madeira wine—a gift from Paddy for his wife's birth day—

hiding in the corner by the pianoforte. Maggie had caught him, yelled in Gaelic as they both watched the decanter tumble, spilling the expensive liquid.

The chains of puce roses on the wallpaper were faded now, the white background faded in areas where the sun shone on it regularly. So many times, one of them had burst into the room with some earth-shattering news, sending the door handle banging against the wall. There was a permanent dent that matched the knob perfectly. Maggie's rocker, always covered with a new blanket when another child was brought to her, needed a new cushion, a bit of sanding (Aonarach had used the bottom rail for teething as a pup), and another coat of varnish.

Yes, the memories in this old parlor—this house—gave him hope he could find happiness like Paddy and Maggie. He'd never forgotten Paddy's words that first day Ben had joined the family.

*Consider this da first day of yer best life, boyo.*

Indeed. Courtesy of the O'Briens.

Ben threw back the rest of his whiskey and stood up, facing Maggie. "Would you care to dance, ma'am?"

Maggie beamed, her round face glowing with happiness and Madeira. "I'd be delighted."

AFTER THE MARRIED couples had left for their respective homes and Maggie had gone to bed, Ben enjoyed a brandy with Paddy, Angus, and Nora.

"We didn't get to finish our earlier conversation,"

said Angus, his black hair gleaming as he sat next to the fire. "Probably a good thing since we aren't supposed to discuss business at the family meal."

"A new client, you said?" asked Ben.

"Yes, you met Lord Tamber at Harry and Mattie's wedding. He hired Eli to do a portrait of his family," said Angus. "Lord Tamber is in search of a solicitor. His father is not doing well, so he may inherit the title of Marquess of Whimberly sooner than expected. He's hesitant to use his father's solicitor as the man is older than the marquess."

Ben nodded. The family had extensive property and investments. As a solicitor, he often oversaw the financial statements for the holdings of his clients. This could be quite a boon for him. If Tamber was happy with Ben's work, there could be more influential members of the *ton*. He might be able to buy a townhouse in the near future rather than years from now.

"Eli liked the man, said he was straightforward and easy to deal with," said Ben.

"Mattie says he has a lovely wife and little boy," added Nora. Harry's wife, Mattie, was the sister of an earl and had known Lord and Lady Tamber socially. "This is a good opportunity for you, Benjie."

Ben smiled at the childhood nickname. Only Nora called him that, and he could never break her of the habit.

Angus leaned forward on his knees, cradling the glass of brandy between his hands. "I would advise against becoming involved with his mother. She's quite the shrew, and from what I understand, a terror to deal with."

"I appreciate the warning," said Ben, wondering how much trouble an old woman could cause. Regardless, the marchioness wasn't hiring him; her son was. But with Angus Marshall's ties to the nobility, Benjamin would take heed of the warning.

Paddy moved on to investigations. "So, where are we with dat Vicar scoundrel? Any rumblings in da legal halls?"

Angus sighed and stood, pacing the room. "One of the guards at Newgate was bribed to let someone in to see Mason. It's a shame, but not unexpected, that no one's talking. If our Harry couldn't dig anything up, my sources certainly won't."

The Vicar was the head of a counterfeit ring—among other illegal ventures—who had been evading the Peelers for several years. Each time they got close to the man—or one of his toadies—a body vanished or turned up dead. Mason had been part of the Vicar's inner circle, but he'd never made it to trial for murder because he'd become a victim himself.

"Mason was finished off quickly and silently. It was the work of a professional, not some henchman," said Nora. "I'd wager it was the same assassin who killed the viscount at Hyde Park last November."

Lord Major Hatfield had been working for the Home Office. He'd informed his superior that he had a lead on where some of the counterfeit banknotes were coming from. But he was injected with poison by a passerby with a loaded parasol and died shortly after.

The newspapers had reported it as a short but lethal illness. It marked the third time poison had been used to eliminate government agents.

"Mason wasn't poisoned," Ben pointed out. "His throat was slit. Though a professional will change his methods depending on the situation."

"We've got the devil on the run, forcing him to take out one of his best men." Paddy slapped his knee. "He'll be irritated with us."

"That's to our advantage," said Angus. "Make his lackeys nervous, not knowing if they're next. They might talk easier."

"I wish we could have spoken with Ruby's father before he jumped on a ship bound for who knows where." Nora shook her head. "Must have been hard on the poor girl, finding out her father worked for such a villain."

"She's safe with Eli and Mrs. Norton now," said Ben, wondering how many other families had been torn apart by The Vicar's influence. "Do you think he'll lie low again? It's his usual next step after eliminating a *liability*."

"Weel, according to my count, da last few years haven't been kind to our Vicar. He's lost four men so far, which don't bode well for trust among da ranks." Paddy scratched his wolfhound's wiry coat, and the dog's back leg began thumping in rhythm. "It takes a long while to earn da kind of trust needed to be in da inner circle. Losing dat many reliable men will leave him vulnerable. So, aye, he'll be scarce again."

"Which means you'll have a little breathing space to

continue the investigation unhindered," said Ben. "Anything new come in?"

Paddy shook his head. "Scheduled an appointment for next week. We'll see what dat brings, but 'tis nice to have a break."

Ben walked along Gracechurch Street, enjoying the exercise and quieter streets at night. He hadn't been to Jackson's in over a week, and he needed to get in the ring. Boxing helped him work out his frustrations. His mind ran over the facts of the O'Brien Investigations' ongoing case with The Vicar, then concentrated on the upcoming meeting with Lord Tamber. He would send a note with his card tomorrow, letting the earl know of his availability.

He paused for several hackneys at the intersection where Cornhill became Leadenhall Street, then continued straight. Another block and Gracechurch switched to Bishopsgate, where Ben lived. When Samson married Dottie, Ben had taken the physician's lodgings. Comfortable with the location—closer to his office—and on good terms with the landlady, it had seemed a good move. There was a mews close by where he could keep a horse, and it wasn't too far from his childhood home, his favorite public houses, and a good meal.

BEN HUMMED AN OLD TAVERN TUNE, a habit of his when he was deep in thought. As he came to a conclusion, the humming usually transformed into a whistle. When they were growing up, his brothers and sister always knew when he was working through a problem. It was Clayton who had pointed out that the whistle always came with a solution. Little things about him that only family would know.

*Family.* Why had he become so sentimental lately? Thinking about family, a wife, children… he wasn't lonely or dissatisfied with his life. It was more of a hole somewhere in the fabric of his life, as if something was missing.

What had Maggie said? He chuckled, remembering her Irish words of wisdom. *Every old sock finds a shoe.*

So was he looking for the sock or the shoe?

# CHAPTER 2

*Monday morning*
*Walbrook Street, Cheapside*

Kitty took the kettle off and poured the steaming water over the leaves, letting the tea steep. "Two pieces of toast or three, Pa?"

"I'm a hungry man, luv. Make it three," called her father from his bedroom. "Any of the marmalade left?"

"Yes, and I bought more hand pies from the butcher." Kitty flipped the bread on the small coal-burning stove that doubled as heat and a place to warm meals. She set the slices in the rack and placed it on the small kitchen table.

Mr. Felton came out of his room, his face red from the recent scrubbing. "Eggs and rashers? What would I do without you?" He kissed her on top of the head and sat down to eat.

Kitty put two warm boiled eggs and thick slices of bacon on a plate and set it before her father. "Anything exciting last night?" She asked the same question every morning, always hoping for the same answer.

"Dull as a tarnished mirror," her father said around a mouthful of pork. "But no rain and mild temperatures."

She smiled. "Good."

"Did you add Mr. Cooper to your route?" he asked, adding a spoonful of the sweet marmalade onto a slice of toast.

"Yes, sir. Thank you for referring me, Pa. This is a wonderful chance for me to bring in an income and still be able to work on my pieces." Kitty dreamed of being a designer. Not a dressmaker, for she hated sewing such big projects. Her accessories had more intricate embroidery and unique materials and embellishments. She and her mother had begun sprucing up old items around the house, and over the years, it had become Kitty's passion.

"More gewgaws?" he asked, accepting a cup of tea. "They're pretty enough, but you need to find a way for the upper class to see them. Our lot won't buy much."

"Our lot is already buying them or bringing me used items to fix up. It's a way to refurbish an old accessory and cheaper than purchasing a new bonnet." She loved her father, but he thought her creations were castles in the air. Nothing would come from them. He indulged her, waiting for the day she'd meet a young man and marry.

"True," he agreed, slurping his tea. "But you need to find a business owner who will display them and not take too much of your profit."

Her father was right, of course. She needed to make a name for herself. The thought of relying on a husband made her stomach tight. Not that she had a bad view of marriage. Her parents had been very happy, and her brother was quite content in the parson's trap. She loved children and wanted some of her own one day.

But having her own blunt, not having to rely on a man for every ha' penny was important to her. And her accessories were something she could still do at home, with children about. She and Mama had made great plans until her mother fell ill two years ago. A fever and cough had racked her body for two weeks before she succumbed to the sickness.

Kitty tossed her wool cloak over her light-brown day dress, then stopped to retie her left boot. The lace was getting thin, and she'd have to purchase new ones soon. She would add the old lace to her basket of odds and ends. One never knew what bits and pieces would come in handy.

"Have I told you lately how proud your mother would be of you?" asked her father, a sheepish expression on his ruddy face.

"Yes, you have, but I don't mind hearing it again." She ran to him and placed a kiss on his cheek and gave him a hug, hoping to remove the regret in his soft brown eyes. "I know you love me, Pa. I feel Mama watching over me, and we'll find a way to make my gewgaws sell."

They both missed her dreadfully, but life did not stop because one's heart was broken.

Cheapside was already busy as she made her way down Walbrook Street. She could hear the vendors calling from Cornhill and Lombard. At the corner, she took a left onto Pancras and stopped at her first house. It was a small printing shop with rented rooms above.

Kitty took out her pea shooter and a few dried peas, popped one of the tiny vegetables into her mouth, and squinted up at the darkened windows. Focusing on the second window on the left, she blew into the slender wooden tube. It pinged against the glass, and she waited several minutes before trying again. If she'd only known when her brother taught her how to do this, that it would become a life skill as an adult.

It took three tries before Mr. Mornay, clerk at a drapery and linen shop, waved at her through the window. She backtracked, ducked up an alley, and came out onto Poultry. This street was already crowded with wagons, carts, and pedestrians shopping for the day's meal. Voices mingled with shouts of the hawkers and dogs barking, the rumble of rickety wheels, and *squish* of mud as boots slopped in and out of the thick muck. It was still muddy from the rain two days ago, and Kitty had to pick up her skirts as she crossed Poultry to take Prince Street over to Throgmorton.

"G'morning," called Mr. Habin, an accountant for the bank, as he opened the window and waved. He was still adjusting his spectacles, and Kitty's hands fidgeted, ready to catch them if the old man dropped them. "Looks like a good day."

"A fine one, indeed. Give the missus my regards," responded Kitty with a smile and a wave. She stopped again on the next block.

"Hello, Mrs. Ranker," Kitty called up to the widow, who was a day cook for a wealthy merchant. "How's your shoulder?"

"Much better," called the round-faced woman. "And your father?"

"Very well, ma'am," she answered back, turning left at the corner onto Broad Street.

She had one stop along here, then proceeded to turn right onto Wormwood. This was a short lane, with the centuries-old houses leaning toward each other like elderly people without their canes. It was darker along the narrow street where the sun struggled to find a path between the slanted buildings.

Kitty reached in and fingered several more dried peas, popping one into her mouth. She counted to the second floor, spotted her target, and blew. And missed.

"Jabbers!" She tried again and hit the pane. Mr. Lockton's drapes opened, and Kitty moved on. He wasn't a social man—not a bad man, by any means, just not much of a conversationalist. So as long as the curtains were pulled back, she knew he was up and about.

Kitty peered into the shadows, searching for the pup she'd seen the last few days. He was a little scruffy terrier mix, gray and brown with a tangled beard. She had brought along a slice of bacon. Squatting next to Mr. Lockton's building, she made a kissing sound and called for the dog.

*Woof!* Then a blur of head, paws, and tail whooshed past her, did an about-face, and looked up at her happily, sitting up pretty. She laughed at his begging pose. Holding the meat above his head, he did several circles on his hind legs before she dropped the treat. His tail wagged furiously as he crunched, and she scratched his wiry coat.

"You're quite the dancer," she cooed to the pup. "I wish I knew if you belonged to someone." She felt along his ribs, knowing in her heart his home was on the streets. He lifted a paw and set it on her arm, his light-brown eyes seeming to look into her soul.

"You are welcome to keep me company," she told him as she resumed her route. To her surprise, he followed behind her at a steady trot.

Turning right onto Bishopsgate, she stopped at her next house. The Miss Fenleys, sisters in their late thirties or early forties, both worked for a seamstress on Bond Street. She blew a pea at the window, and the dog added a *woof*.

"Hello, Kitty," called the elder sister, her curly blonde hair still stuffed under a mob cap. "Who is your friend?"

Kitty peered at the dog next to her feet. "We've only met a few days ago. He doesn't have a name."

"Not yet? I'm sure you'll come up with something that fits him," said the younger Miss Fenley, poking her head over her sister's shoulder. "He's very dirty. What about Muddy?"

"Muddy?" snapped the elder Fenley. "That's a ridiculous name."

"Well, do you have a better one?" groused the other sister.

"No, but..."

Kitty walked away smiling, the voices of the two siblings fading. Every morning, they began the day bickering over something. Yet everyone knew they were devoted to each other.

She checked the houses as she walked, looking for the direction of her new client. When she found the boarding house, she double-checked the number, found his window, and shot a dried pea right in the middle of the pane. And waited. The pup let out a bark. She drew out another pea and hit her target again. The curtain pulled back, and a handsome blond man's face appeared.

She held up a hand to acknowledge he was awake, and he did the same. Walking away, Kitty looked over her shoulder to see Mr. Cooper still watching her. Warmth spread through her, and she smiled to herself.

"My, I think he should be at the beginning of my route. What a lovely way to start my day," she said to the terrier. "He's quite..."

The dog barked again. "Exactly," she agreed.

THE NEXT MORNING, Pa announced, "Your canine friend is waiting for you."

"What?"

Her father held the door open to reveal the pup sitting outside. "You might as well come in and get something to eat. I know she's been feeding you on her rounds," he told the dog. "A smart dog always knows a soft heart when it sees one."

Kitty grinned and squatted to call the dog to her. "Terry, come!"

"You've named him already?" Pa shook his head. "I should have known. I'm surprised a dozen mutts haven't followed you home since you started waking people."

"For your information, I just came up with the name." Kitty planted her fists on her hips, playfully indignant. "He's a terrier, so Terry will suit him."

"Yes, it will. I suppose we should pull out the basket?" Her father raised a dark, graying brow.

"You kept it?" she asked, surprised.

Her mother had brought home a stray when Kitty was ten. Buford had been some kind of hound dog, and as he grew, he began going with her father on his night watch. Buford had slept in a large basket next to the stove, and she'd seen the tears in Pa's eyes the night Buford thumped his tail but didn't get up to accompany his beloved owner. A few weeks later, the hound had passed in the night. Both the hound and basket had disappeared that morning, and Kitty never had the heart to ask her father about them. That was six months ago.

"We've had a dog most of your life," he said. "I'd feel better if you had someone, er something, with you when you go out. If you continue this through the winter, the mornings will still be dark."

Kitty threw her arms around her father's neck. "Thank you, Pa."

Her heart was light as she made her rounds with Terry on her heels. When she came to Mr. Cooper's home, she cursed the wings taking flight in her stomach. Once again, he pulled back a curtain, and they both waved in acknowledgment.

THE WEEK WENT BY QUICKLY, and Terry soon knew her route as well as she did. Kitty had begun creating a fantasy around the handsome solicitor. In one daydream, he was a man in a mask and dark cape, riding on horseback to save her. In another, he was a pirate who stole her from a ship and made her his accomplice bride. Yesterday, he was a prince in hiding, escaping the duties of his royal family.

"I should be a novelist with my imagination," she confided to the terrier. "I've turned a dull solicitor into an adventurer without ever holding a conversation with him." Terry barked his agreement.

They left the Miss Fenleys, and she stopped again to pull two dried peas from her pocket. She had worked up a sweat playing with Terry, running back and forth in the alley as he chased her. She pushed back her hood to allow the breeze to cool her neck and face. When she reached Mr. Cooper's house, she was surprised to see him at the window before she could even pop a pea in her mouth.

He lifted the sash and leaned out. "Good morning, Miss Felton." He had a wonderful smile, white teeth, and blond hair that was sticking up in several directions.

She giggled. "Good morning, Mr. Cooper."

"Who is your helper?" he asked, nodding at the dog.

"This is Terry. He's new and still in training," she said with a grin, appreciating the opportunity to study this man more closely. His eyes were the color of honey, a golden brown, and she found it hard to look away.

"Is he a fast learner?" asked Mr. Cooper, that smile sending her stomach into a tumble despite the tousled hair.

"He is, but the pea shooter is giving him a bit of trouble. I think it's the lack of fingers," she said, gazing up at the window. She pushed a hand through her black waves self-consciously and noticed his eyes widened. Was her hair mussed too?

"The what?" His brows furrowed, then understanding smoothed them as she pulled out her tool of the trade. "Ah, I remember using one of those when I was a boy. A lack of hands would definitely hurt Terry's progress."

"Yes, I'm afraid I won't be able to let him go on his own until he masters it," she said, her tone serious. "However, his accompanying bark after I shoot does seem to be helpful."

Mr. Cooper laughed. A warm, welcoming sound like a hot toddy on a cold day. "Well, thank you for the knock up."

"You're very welcome," she said, watching him lower the sash.

As she walked away, she heard him exclaim, "Bollocks."

# CHAPTER 3

*Bishopsgate*

Ben stared at his reflection in the mirror, trying to smooth down the points of hair taunting him. For the love of saints, why hadn't he checked his appearance before sticking his head out the window.

*How was I to know?*

Yesterday, he'd caught a jarring glimpse of Miss Felton. Very pretty from what he'd seen. All this time, he assumed "my Kitty" was Felton's wife. If this raven-haired prime article wasn't his daughter, then Ben had misjudged the night watchman. So today, he thought he'd get a better look. With a sigh of disgust, he splashed water on his face and rubbed his hair before taking a comb to it.

She had hair the color of midnight, and eyes that

weren't quite blue. Violet, if he had to put a color to them. A striking combination. His belly tightened as he remembered her alabaster skin and lovely smile. And he engaged her with his hair looking as if he'd just rolled out of bed.

Well, he had, of course, which was why she was stopping below his room every morning. Still...

He'd do better tomorrow. Ben paused, wondering why he cared what he looked like to a young girl, a stranger.

He did know her father, in a way. They were acquaintances, at least.

*Admit it. She's stunning with a winsome smile. And she has a sense of humor.*

Ben was intrigued. He wasn't a man influenced by beauty, though not immune to it. She and her canine friend made a charming picture. Yes, it was a good decision hiring Miss Felton.

* * *

*Chancery Lane*

Benjamin stood to shake hands with Lord Tamber. "It's been a pleasure, my lord," he said to the earl. "I'll prepare the contract and complete the rest of the documents for your signature."

"Excellent. I'm fortunate to have run into Mr. Marshall at White's and have him suggest you," said the earl, placing his beaver hat upon his dark, wavy hair. "I hope I don't seem as if I'm anticipating my father's death. I just want to be prepared and make the transition as smooth as possible when it does happen."

"Unfortunately, death is inevitable. It's prudent to plan ahead," agreed Ben. "May I ask what ails him?"

"Heart. Our physician said my father could be around another ten years or be gone tomorrow. He had a frightening episode that left him in bed for the better part of a month." Lord Tamber smiled. "Though he seems right enough now. Insists he'll outlive me and my brother."

"Let's hope he's with us for years to come."

"Yes, it's hard to imagine the country estate without him, though he hasn't taken his seat in the Lords for several years." The earl gave Ben a nod. "Good day, then, Mr. Cooper. Give my regards to Mr. Norton."

"That's right, my brother Elijah did a portrait for you. I hope you were pleased?"

"Very much so," said the earl, stopping at the door. "In fact, I'd like him to paint my mother."

Ben held back a cringe at those words, remembering the recent warning about the woman. Perhaps Angus had been exaggerating, or Eli's gentle nature would win the marchioness over.

After several hours of research, paperwork, and going over client ledgers, he leaned back in his chair and yawned, his arms stretched above his head. He checked his pocket watch. Almost half past five. He was meeting Roger Lynch at the Dog's Bone at six-thirty. Just enough time to finish up.

Ben walked along Chancery Lane until he reached

Holborn and hailed a hackney. He gave the direction to the Dog's Bone and leaned back against the worn leather squab. With responsibilities finished for the day, he let his mind wander. It wasn't surprising that flowing black hair and purplish-blue eyes soon filled his thoughts.

It wasn't like him to be preoccupied with a woman. He hadn't been smitten since boyhood when a neighbor girl had flirted with him. She'd given him his first kiss under the tree in the backyard. It had fueled his dreams for weeks.

*Don't be a bufflehead. She's just a girl, probably too young anyway.*

At the Dog's Bone, Ben waved at Max, the balding barkeep and owner, and exchanged smiles with Martha. The owner's wife had a cherubic face with cheeks that were always flushed and sandy-brown hair usually stuffed into a mobcap.

"He's waitin' for ye in the back," she said, nodding toward the storeroom and Max's office. "I'll let Bess know you're here. Got some hand pies left over from earlier if you want one."

"Two, please," Ben said, giving her a forlorn look.

"Those beggin' tawny eyes get me ever' time." She pushed him toward the back, and he maneuvered his way through the evening crowd.

The back room was dark, only a small hearth providing light, and looked much like it probably had two hundred years ago. Shelves lined the stone walls, and overhead, low charred timbers from years of smoke forced most of patrons to duck whenever they entered. Ben's heels clicked on the flagstone as he joined Roger Lynch at the table in the center of the room. A fire in the hearth crackled cheerfully behind him, and bread and cheese sat on a table along one wall. The far wall was an alcove with the best of Max's brandy and ale.

"You look tired," said Roger, his grayish-green eyes teasing.

"Thank you, and you look like the cat who ate the canary." Ben sat down across from Roger. "Good news, I hope?"

Roger was the second latecomer to the O'Brien clan. Harry Walters had come across the lad being set upon by footpads a couple years back. Roger had valiantly held them off from plucking his mother's rent money but was fast losing the fight. Harry assisted in making the odds a bit more even, then brought the lad to the O'Briens to get him fixed up. He'd been working for the family ever since. Newly eighteen, he was a handsome young man with a thick mane of black curly hair and a wicked punch that had earned him respect with Paddy's Peelers.

"I'm on the trail of Eli's father. Got a good lead today from one of my more trusted sources." Roger grinned, obviously pleased with himself. "I think we'll keep it to ourselves, though, until I get closer."

"I'd hate to disappoint Eli," agreed Ben. Eli's father had married Eli's mother when he already had a wife. After confessing, he'd left them both, and Eli had never seen him again.

Clayton Pierce burst through the door, green eyes blazing. "Hey ho," he cried, slamming a bumper of ale in front of Ben, the contents slopping over the side onto the scarred oak. "Bess is bringing your pies. Did I miss anything?"

Ben rolled his eyes while Roger repeated the news. He was closest to Clayton out of all his brothers, and he envied the man his natural vivacity and charm. He hated to admit it, but Ben had been relieved when Clayton had found Genie, his fiancée. They would marry next month.

"That's demmed excellent!" Clay pulled the cap from his auburn hair. "Well done, Lynch."

Roger beamed at the praise. "Eli's left Bow Street, and I started last week."

First a man of all jobs for the O'Briens, he was now part of the investigative team. One of the requirements to be a Peeler was experience as a Runner. Ben knew Roger would shine. He was clever, hardworking, and loyal.

"How's Miss Chapelle?" asked Ben. "I assume she is making her own dress?"

"Miss Chapelle?" Clayton rolled his eyes.

"I'm still on solicitor manners. How is Genie, then?"

"I don't know how a woman can spend so much time with a needle," said Clayton, shaking his head.

"Because she's a modiste, and it's how she earns a wage?" asked Ben, arching one brow. "Will she continue running her shop with her aunt after you're married?"

"Can you imagine me telling her no?" A sheepish

smile covered Clayton's face. "She's already said that, even when she's with child, she can still wield a needle and thread."

Ben slapped his brother on the back as the three men laughed. Clayton was another reason Ben had decided to consider marriage. He'd never seen Pierce this content, this satisfied with his life. Ben envied him —and Sam and Harry.

"I've been lurking," began Clayton, waving the old wool cap in the air to indicate part of his disguise. "It seems with The Vicar's top men falling from grace—or the gallows—there is some fighting over who will move up."

"With the way he's losing trusted men, I'd think they'd run the other way," said Roger. "The odds don't seem to favor being next to the boss."

"Exactly what the problem is. No one wants to be the next martyr. A couple of them are even trying to find a way out." He paused as Bess entered with Ben's meal. The pretty barmaid scanned their faces, disappointment on her face. "Sorry, luv, Gus isn't coming tonight."

She shoved a brown curl into her mobcap and thrust her chin out. "Why should I care whether he comes or goes?" Which they all knew was a big fat whisker. It was no secret that Bess held a torch for Gus, who could think of no other woman except Nora. But the triangle did not close since Nora only loved Gus as a brother.

Once they were alone again, Clayton continued, "I

suspect the two who want to try a different path will soon be floating in the Thames. No one walks away from The Vicar's congregation."

"What a lovely thing to look forward to," groaned Roger. "I heard he knows about the Peelers being involved."

Clayton nodded. "Afraid so. We'll have to be more careful. Seems our friend Rowlands wants to be the next napper to replace Mason. Harry will be indispensable with his talent for disguises. I've actually run into him before and not recognized him."

Ben licked his fingers and finished the first pie. The crust was flaky with just the right amount of crunch. The steak and kidney mixed into the rich brown gravy dripped onto the plate. He dipped the corner of the second pie into the brown puddle and took another bite. "The sooner his identity is discovered, the safer London will be."

Later that night, lying in bed, Ben wondered about the villain the Peelers had chased for so long. They knew he had his fingers in several pots, the largest—that they knew of—was counterfeiting. The forged banknotes had surfaced outside of Great Britain, returning to the London banks from India. A place where the Crown had interests and investments. But who had received them first and from whom?

Angus discovered the payees on the notes were difficult to track down, so they were most likely aliases. So a man accepting the counterfeit notes had to have an accomplice within a bank in order to cash them.

Had those taking the notes known they were counterfeit? Or were they given as bribes for some reason?

His eyes drooped close, and soon, he was dreaming of a beautiful Indian girl with black hair and deep-violet eyes. She wore a colorful sarong that clung to her body, dancing in slow undulations, her long graceful arms beckoning. There were bangles on her wrists that clinked as she moved.

*Woof!*

He peered on either side of the beautiful woman, looking for a dog. Was it part of the performance?

*Pop!*

*Woof!*

He opened his eyes with a smile on his face, then realized the sound had come from the window. He threw back the counterpane and dashed to the window, throwing up the sash just as the little terrier let out another bark.

"You were sleeping sound, Mr. Cooper," said Miss Felton, smiling up at him. "I thought I might have to ask the landlady to knock on your door."

Gazing down on her, Ben's mind redressed her in the clothes she'd worn in his dreams. Heat rushed through him, both desire and embarrassment coloring his cheeks. "I was in the middle of a dream, but the dog's bark was misplaced. I think it's what woke me up."

"Are you feeling well? Do you usually sleep so hard?" she asked.

Ben shook his head. "No, I don't think so. But I'll

continue to pay you the extra just in case it happens again."

He knew he wore a ridiculous grin on his face, but he couldn't seem to stop. Then he noticed her eyes were darting from his eyes to his hair and back. She chewed her bottom lip as if holding back a laugh. He ran a hand through his hair and closed his eyes.

*Not again.* Why did he have such bad luck?

"I must insist we meet during the day at least once. So you'll know what I look like without disheveled hair." Then the absurd smile returned. He needed to end this conversation before he made more of a fool of himself. "I swear I own a comb. Here, I'll show you."

He ducked from the window and grabbed the horn comb next to his basin and waved it at her.

So much for quitting before he made a fool of himself. Miss Felton only smiled placatingly, probably wondering about the numbskull man who had just hired her. If she was an intelligent girl, she'd run as fast as she could. Who knows what imbecile things he would do or say tomorrow.

Terry barked, his tail wagging furiously as his mistress tried to quiet him. At least the dog liked him.

"I don't expect anyone to look their best when I'm waking them," she said, mischief in those purplish-blue eyes. "I'm sure you're a swell once your day has begun."

"But not handsome?" Why did he just put her on the spot like that? Yes, he was well-dressed for his clients, but swell didn't include his face.

She laughed, and the sound put the grin back on his face. "I'm sure you're that too. Good day, Mr. Cooper."

Then she whistled to her dog and practically ran down the street.

He should go back to bed and stay there for the day. Wait for her to come again tomorrow and try again. Or leave the poor woman alone before he frightened her off, and he was left to the devices of his landlady.

# CHAPTER 4

*A week later*
*Walbrook Street*

Kitty opened the door at the sound of scratching. Terry stood on the other side, his little tail moving at the speed of a fast carriage wheel. Her father was still farther down the street.

"Did you keep him company?" she asked the dog.

*Woof!*

He had begun following Pa to the door at night and was soon a companion for him as well. Kitty decided her father couldn't change his mind about keeping the pup if he was earning his keep.

As her father entered, he bent to pet the dog. "He's a good 'un," said Pa. "He walks ahead of me and barks if there's someone down an alley. Gives me warning if there's anything I should pay attention to."

Kitty beamed. "I'm glad you're happy with him too. I feel better when someone is with you." The area her father patrolled wasn't a rookery, but their neighborhood was no Mayfair either. There were bad people everywhere, as her mother used to say.

"Wouldn't you rather have him with you at night when you're alone?"

She shook her head. "Nah, Widower Mercer upstairs would hear me yell. He'd come down quick enough if I needed help." Kitty would never say how much she'd love to have Terry with her in the evening. Besides, she'd slept better this week, knowing the dog accompanied her father.

"Is the young solicitor still making cow eyes at you?"

"It's strange how the first week he didn't give me any notice but a wave." Setting the steeped tea on the table, she sat down and began buttering a slice of bread. "Then one day, he poked his head out the window, and he's full of prittle prattle. We speak for a few minutes every day, but he's not such a flat anymore. He's terrible at jokes, but I laugh so as not to hurt his feelings."

"Still trying to impress you, then," said her father with a knowing smile.

"His hair *is* combed now when he comes to the window," she said with a chuckle.

"I like Mr. Cooper. He's respectful and makes a good living, I think. Comes from a good family."

"You know some Coopers?" she asked.

"Naw, he was raised by the O'Briens. Paddy was a

Runner for years—that's how we met—and he and his wife raised a whole brood of castoffs." Pa picked up his fork and dug into his eggs and rashers, tossing a piece of meat to Terry. "All seven of them have made something of themselves."

"Seven?" Her mouth fell open. "They took in seven waifs?"

He nodded, reaching for the bread as Kitty pushed the bowl of butter toward him. "The missus couldn't bear a child, so they found another way to have a family. You'd like them. Nice Irish couple."

Her mind was still catching up with raising seven children from different backgrounds.

"Remember me talking about Dr. Brooks? He's part of that family. When he married, Mr. Cooper took his rooms." Pa dropped a crust of bread for Terry.

"From orphan to physician? That's quite impressive."

She had assumed Mr. Cooper had come from a well-off family who sent him to university. It had never occurred to her that he might be an orphan. She smiled, feeling proud of him for some reason.

"Careful out there this morning," Pa said around a mouthful of eggs. "Some thick pea soup and no sun to dissipate it. The alleys are still dark."

The heavy fog was more than a nuisance. It could be toxic to those with weak lungs, like her mother. A pea-souper was a rancid yellow combination of fog and smoke. It often smelled of chemicals and could be so dense that it was hard to see the ground.

"I'll wear my hooded cloak and cover my head," she

said. After finishing her tea, she carried her plates to the dry sink and set them in a large basin. "I'll finish the kitchen when I return."

"Good girl. Better to leave early and keep your eyes peeled. Some of those drivers don't bother to slow down in conditions like these." He turned to the dog. "Let her know if you hear wheels coming around a corner."

Terry barked a *yes*, and when Kitty reached for her forest-green pelisse, he went to the door and waited. She checked her pockets, then decided to grab more dried peas. Hurrying to the cupboard, she grabbed a tin, opened it, and poured a handful into her palm. A few spilled on the floor. "Jabbers," she cursed as she hurried to pick them up before Terry ate them.

It was a chilly morning for April, the sodden air making the fog cling to her boots. She pulled up the hood to keep the moisture from her hair. The day was dreary, and Kitty desperately wanted to finish her route and get back to her warm home. She had mending to do waiting next to the rocker by the stove. Terry would curl up next to her and sleep between his shifts, as Pa called them.

The yellow vapor still hadn't dissipated by the time they turned the corner onto Wormwood. The narrow street was shadowy at the best time of day, but now, Kitty paused and squinted into the murky lane. Terry growled.

"There's nothing to see, silly dog. Why are you growling?" She bent to scratch his ears, then moved forward. After waking Mr. Lockton, barely seeing his curtain fling open, Kitty breathed a sigh of relief. She had an eerie feeling, and watching the scruff on Terry's neck rise didn't help.

Near the end of the lane, before the buildings stopped leaning so much and daylight could be seen, Kitty saw a dark form. A man or a woman?

Shouting erupted. Definitely two male voices. Kitty slowed her pace, hoping they would move on. She was so close to Bishopsgate. As she drew near the man, still arguing with someone in the alley, a hand struck out and grabbed the man by the throat, pulling him out of sight.

Kitty screamed, and Terry began growling again. *Run,* screamed a voice in head. *Run!*

She obeyed, picking up her skirts and making a dash for the corner. But as she passed the alley, her feet seemed to move in slow motion. A body lay on the ground, and another man wearing a neckcloth over his face stood over him. As the standing man looked over his shoulder, his gaze locked with Kitty's. The fog shifted around his head like a gothic portrait, briefly showing his face. The cloth fell to his chin, and Kitty could just make out a short beard. A large pale scar zigzagged down the side of his face, disappearing under the facial hair.

Something flashed in his hand. A knife. The stranger moved quickly toward her, and panic froze her to the spot until Terry began barking. The tough little terrier charged the man. Kitty grabbed the folds of her pelisse and skirts and ran as fast as she could.

Behind her, a deep voice cursed as the growling

grew louder. She heard a sharp cry—her dog—then silence. When she got to the Fenley sisters' house, she sat on the front step to catch her breath.

And burst into tears.

Kitty wanted to go back for Terry, but she was terrified to run into the man again. A man who might have just murdered someone. She sat for a moment, her face in her hands, sobbing. Until a warm tongue licked her knuckles. She peeked between her fingers, and Terry kissed her eyes.

The relief sent her into a giggling, hiccupping episode, sweeping Terry into her arms and hugging him as she rocked back and forth. She stayed there until the trembling eased.

"You might have saved my life, and I deserted you," she mumbled into his thick coat. "I'm sorry, Terry. I'm so sorry."

The dog licked her again, his tail thumping against her leg.

"I'm glad you don't hold a grudge. I promise never to desert you again," she whispered in his ear. "Let's finish this and get home. Pa will know what to do."

The sisters appeared behind her, wrapped in robes, mobcaps askew on their heads.

"We heard you crying," said the elder sister. "Are you all right?"

Kitty nodded, not sure what to say. If she was a witness to something foul, she didn't want to involve the Fenleys.

"Oh my dear," said the younger sister, "you're shaking. Goodness, were you almost hit? Days like this always bring a few casualties from those wild drivers."

"People are always in such a hurry," admonished the elder sister. "Life goes fast enough, I say. Slow down and enjoy it before it's too late."

As the Fenleys discussed the dangers of traffic and bad drivers, Kitty was able to collect herself. Assuring them she was fully recovered and fine physically, Kitty bade them good day.

One more stop.

This morning, she would not tarry with Mr. Cooper. She wanted to be home with her father, his big, strong arms around her, telling her all would be well. When the solicitor opened the sash and leaned out, she waved and abruptly left. His confused expression at her change in routine almost made her turn around to explain. But her fear won out.

Kitty ran the rest of the way home, Terry on her heels. She burst into their small set of rooms, shouting for her father. He came from his room, rubbing his reddened eyes.

"What is it, luv? You're white as a ghost," said Pa.

"I think I saw the making of one."

# CHAPTER 5

*Next day*
*Bishopsgate*

Ben's brain was tired from the multitude of figures and documents he had perused throughout the day. Lord Tamber's property and investments were significant, but nothing compared to the holdings from the title he would inherit. The marquess had agreed that Ben should be familiar with his lands and dealings, so Ben had spent the afternoon with the aging solicitor.

It had been a pleasant day, but his eyes were dry from reading so much small print and the shaky handwriting of the older solicitor. He wanted to put a warm cloth on them and sip a good brandy. A perfect end to the day.

"Mr. Cooper."

Ben stopped on the steps of the boarding house and looked over his shoulder to see Mr. Felton walking toward him with purpose. The night watchman's face was drawn and lacked the usual jovial expression.

"Mr. Cooper, I need your help. Can we speak somewhere in private?"

"Of course, my place is right up here. My landlady has a small parlor where we can entertain guests." Ben led the way, wondering what on earth the man could want.

Once inside, he informed Mrs. Meyer that they would be using the parlor. Ben kept a decanter of brandy on the sideboard. He poured two glasses and handed one to Mr. Felton, who accepted it with a shaky hand.

"I'm afraid my Kitty has gotten into a bit of trouble," Mr. Felton began, his pathetic attempt at a half smile making him look almost comical. "We need some guidance on the matter."

Benjamin blinked, then nodded for the man to continue, his own thoughts whirling. *That lovely girl into trouble?* His first thought was someone had hurt her, and anger unfurled in his chest. Then he decided it must be something else, or Mr. Felton would have taken care of it. *What could she have possibly done?*

"I believe she witnessed a murder early this morning while making her rounds." Mr. Felton threw back the expensive brandy.

Ben did the same, grabbing the decanter and pouring them both another one. Was that why Miss

Felton had run off so quickly this morning without a word? "Was she hurt?"

"No, by the grace of God. The dog intervened, giving her time to run." The night watchman ran a steadier hand through his dark, graying mane. "The pup's been coming with me at night—good company, he is—but I left him with her this evening. I didn't want her to be alone."

"Have you gone to the constable?" Ben had an inkling that was why Mr. Felton was here. Even in his position as a Charley, like many people, he was leery of going to the authorities.

"No, not yet. I was thinking it would be better if she just lays low for a spell and pretended like it didn't happen. At least until we found out what element was involved." Mr. Felton's light-brown eyes pleaded for understanding. "Don't want to be involved as a witness if it's someone powerful. I'd go mad as a March hare if something happened to my little girl."

"How old is she?" His logical mind was already whirring with the possibility she could be a witness to a crime.

"She's not but nineteen. Well, twenty next July."

With a loud sigh, Ben sat down in one of the leather wingback chairs. "I understand your reluctance to go to the constable." He immediately thought of The Vicar and the unrest in his ranks.

"I thought, as one of Mr. O'Brien's brood, you might be able to find out if there's been a murder on Wormwood and what kind of danger a witness might be in. Kitty's ready to report it, but I held her back."

Ben couldn't blame the man. He'd be wary too if someone he loved was in the same position. Clayton's fiancée had witnessed a murder. They had been able to use her statement without revealing her identity since the villain had never been found. She had also been hidden in a carriage and not seen. "Let me see what I can find out. In the meantime, could you arrange for me to speak with her? Perhaps bring along one of my brothers?"

Mr. Felton's shoulders slumped with relief. "I thank you from the bottom of my heart. We want to do what's right, but I can't jeopardize my family."

"Of course not, and I would do the same in your position." He sipped his brandy, enjoying the smooth heat as it slid down his throat. "Tell me what you know."

Mr. Felton repeated the story his daughter had told him that morning. "I'm telling her customers she's got a chill, and I'll wake them until further notice. She's spittin' mad about that, but I can't let her out. That villain is surely looking for her."

"He may not know how much she saw. He may not have even realized the mask had slipped from his face. But I agree, it's better to be cautious." Logic told him the opposite, but he didn't want to scare the man any more than he already was.

"I'll give you my direction on Walbrook, and you can stop by in the morning if you'd like," said Mr. Felton, standing. "I need to be off. Thank you, Mr. Cooper. You don't know how much it means to me."

"I'll be ready at the time Miss Felton usually comes

by, and we'll walk to your home together." Ben shook the man's hand. "Then I'll speak with Paddy and my brothers and see what we can discover."

He was restless that night, unable to sleep. Punching his feather pillow, he closed his eyes and took in deep breaths, trying to clear his mind of the conversation with Mr. Felton and the images of "my Kitty." When he finally drifted off, it was well past midnight.

*Ben paused on the slick cobblestone, listening to footsteps echoing in the alley. No one was in front or behind him, yet he heard their presence. He saw a flash of green from the corner of his eye and spun in that direction, walking swiftly toward the street. As he reached the end of the alley, he saw the hem of the green coat disappear around the corner, and he hurried after it.*

*When he followed the cloaked figure into another alley. The fog was thick, but he saw the person stop. She let out a shrill scream.*

*"Wait," Ben yelled to her, knowing it was Miss Felton confronting the murderer.*

*She turned at the sound of his voice, and he saw the fear in her luminous violet eyes. The man behind her placed an arm around her chest and held a knife to her throat.*

*"Don't come any closer, or I'll have to take care of you too," the stranger rasped as he pulled Miss Felton backwards with him.*

*Ben ran toward them, but the urgency and panic caused him to stumble. He fell face down against the slimy ground, his fingers digging into the dirt as he tried to rise quickly. The alley was a dead-end, yet they were nowhere in sight.*

*His head swiveled back and forth, looking for a door or opening where they might have escaped.*

*He leaned against the damp brick of a building, hands on his knees as he caught his breath. A figure towered over him, and he heard the anguished voice of Mr. Felton.*

*"You said this wouldn't happen. You would keep her safe if she told what she witnessed."*

*Ben shook his head. "I tried—"*

*A scream rang through the alley.*

Ben sat up in bed, dragging air into his lungs. Dawn cast a light glow across the floor. It had only been a dream—a nightmare, actually. He would get dressed and meet Mr. Felton, speak with his daughter, then figure out the best course of action. This was a case for the Peelers if there ever had been. And he knew his brothers would be ready to help.

# CHAPTER 6

*Walbrook Street*

"Now take a deep breath, close your eyes, and think back to yesterday morning. Every detail that comes to you. Sometimes it's the smallest memory that is the most important." Mr. Cooper sat across from her with his elbows on the table, his hands folded as he spoke to her softly.

Kitty nodded, hoping she could maintain her composure as she did what he asked. It had been the longest night of her life, waiting for her father to come home. She had slept with Terry, curling herself around the dog, needing the warmth of another body close.

"Terry and I were on Wormwood. It's an old, narrow street with ancient buildings that look like they're ready to topple. It was a pea-souper yesterday morning, and I was running a bit late because of it.

The lane was dark because of the fog." Kitty took a sip of her tea and swallowed, smiling weakly at her father when he patted her other hand. Terry lay at her feet.

"I'd just woke Mr. Lockton when I heard two men arguing. Farther down the lane, I saw one man yelling and waving his arms at another who was in the alley and out of sight. As we got closer, I saw a gloved hand reach out and grab the man's neck, pulling him into the alley."

Kitty closed her eyes again as she remembered the fear that had frozen her next. "I waited a moment, and when I didn't hear anything, I figured they went into one of the buildings off the alley." She wrapped her hands around the teacup, hoping to still the trembling.

"So you continued walking toward the alley?" prompted Mr. Cooper gently.

She nodded. "As I passed it, I saw one man standing over another, a blade in his hand. When he looked at me over his shoulder, fear froze me to the spot. Then he started toward me, and Terry began growling, and I ran. I thought Terry would follow me, but he went after the stranger." Tears slid down her cheeks, and she dashed them away. "I heard the dog whine, and I thought he was dead."

Terry put a paw on her leg, his tail thumping against her boot, and let out a mournful howl. Her father pulled his chair closer and wrapped his arms around her. "It's all right, luv. Mr. Cooper is going to help us figure this out."

"I will do everything possible to find who these men

are and what possible threat they could be to you," answered Mr. Cooper.

Pa handed her his handkerchief, and she took it, wiping her face, then blowing her nose. She peeked at the handsome blond solicitor over the cloth. The kindness in his tawny eyes almost set her to weeping again.

"I'm sorry you're involved in this," she said with a sniffle. "My father was adamant we speak to you first. He's worried the man might come after me."

"Can you describe him? I realize the fog made it difficult, but anything will help," asked Mr. Cooper, opening a small notebook, a pencil in one hand.

"He was tall… lean. He wore dark clothing and a neckcloth around his face. But it had slipped to his chin. I saw a dark beard, or he was unshaved. So dark hair, I assume, but he wore a cap. When he got closer, it was his scar that stood out. A long, jagged scar down the side of his face." She shivered.

"You were able to see his face even with the fog?" Ben finished writing and looked up at her.

"I can't say I saw all his features clearly—just the beard and that scar." She shivered again, remembering his gaze so void of emotion. "He'd just stabbed a man, and he seemed so… calm."

"Which side?"

Kitty stared at him a moment, then realized what he was asking. "The right side of his face."

"Do you think you could identify the man if you saw him again?"

She shrugged, uncertain. "I'd know that scar. That moment will haunt me until I'm old and gray."

"Well, that's the plan," said Mr. Cooper, then rushed on. "I mean, not for anything to haunt you but to see you grow old and gray."

Kitty smiled, the weight on her chest easing. "Thank you, Mr. Cooper."

He opened his mouth to say something, then seemed to change his mind. Instead, he rose from the chair and tucked away his notebook. "If I learn anything, I will return tomorrow morning or tell you, Mr. Felton. In the meantime, I'm in agreement that you should remain out of sight."

"Do you think I'm in danger?" she asked, the knot in her stomach tightening. His hesitation told her all she needed to know. Yes, she was.

"I believe we should stay on the side of caution until we learn who the victim was. It could have been a footpad setting on a random passerby. If so, I doubt very much he would waste too much time searching for you, Miss Felton. He'll assume you would prefer to stay out of it."

But his tone carried concern. His honey-brown eyes held hers, and for a moment, she thought he would reach out and touch her. In comfort?

Pa walked the solicitor to the door, Terry standing next to the opening, ready to follow the older man out. But he shut the door after thanking Mr. Cooper again, then returned to sit at the table.

"I think we did the right thing, Kitty," said her father, though his doubtful tone didn't match his words. "The Peelers have an excellent reputation. If anyone can help us, it's them."

"I hate for you to take my route for me," she said, despising the thought of being cooped up for days, though she had been able to create two new bonnets yesterday.

"I don't mind, luv," he said, then cleared his throat as he sat back down. "I think it would be best for you to stay with your brother until we know you are safe."

Kitty knew from his eyes that he expected a fight. "I don't know if either man saw me waking Mr. Lockton. If they did, the murderer can easily find out who I am. I wouldn't be any safer with Joe, and we would put his wife in danger."

Her father sighed loudly. "You're right. I'm not thinking." He put his head in his hands. "I admit I'm cold right down to my soul, worried for you."

She went to him and wrapped an arm around his shoulder, returning the comfort he'd recently given her. "We'll get through this, Pa. We've been through worse—think of Mama."

He nodded, took in a ragged breath, and met her gaze. "We have, haven't we? And this will be a grand adventure you can tell to your babes someday."

Kitty cleaned their rooms before her father went to bed, then took out her basket of bits, a short claret-colored pelisse of sturdy cotton, and a matching pair of gloves. As she worked, trying this paste jewel, different lace, or sequins, her mind returned to the frightening scar and where she might stay to keep danger at bay from both herself and her family.

Her lids grew heavy, and she moved to the rocker to rest her eyes for just a moment. An image of Mr.

Cooper filled her head, his sweet smile, the concerned dark-gold eyes, the thick blond hair—combed nicely today. That thought made her smile. Her first of the day.

Would he be able to protect them? Perhaps he could find her a place to hide away. There was something strong and solid about the solicitor. Kitty inexplicably knew she would be safe with Mr. Cooper. Physically.

But her heart? She wasn't so sure.

# CHAPTER 7

*The Dog's Bone*

"We've go' a fine roasted fowl with parsnips and peas," said Bess, watching Gus out of the corner of her eye. "Anyone interested?"

Ben hid his smile. "Sounds good, Bess. Thank you."

"I'll take a plate too. Mum only cooks a meal once, and I'll be late tonight," said Roger Lynch, giving the lass a wink and laughing when she blushed. Gus glared at him.

When the pretty barmaid had left the back office, Roger's smoky green eyes turned on Gus. "You're right dull, considerin' how smart you are."

Gus pulled his cap off his dark hair and ran a hand through the tangles. He growled at the young man. "What the devil is that s'posed to mean?"

"Instead of pinin' after the woman who *doesn't* love

you—like that," Roger added quickly when Gus rose to his full height and hovered over the boy.

August Rutland was a huge man, as big as Paddy, and as good with his fists as he was with a pistol. His dark-brown hair was unfashionably long and always pulled back with a leather thong.

"Bess is smelling of April and May when she looks at you, and you break her heart every time," Roger continued undaunted. "Maybe I'll try wooin' her."

Gus rolled his dark eyes. "She doesn't want me, so stop yer Banbury tales before my fist ends up in yer mouth."

"In a foul mood, ain't we?" asked Clayton with a grin. He was dressed in homespun wool, slightly tattered, a brown cap set rakishly on his auburn hair. He was still undercover with a gang of men working for The Vicar. "The truth does that to a man."

Gus picked up his ale, gulped it down, and slammed it on the table. "Sorry, Lynch. I'm hungry, and it's been a fruitless day."

Roger grinned. "It's all right. I know you like me."

Gus grunted while Clayton snorted, his green eyes sparkling with humor.

"Have there been any murders reported in my neighborhood? Maybe an alley off Wormwood?" asked Ben, getting to the point.

All three stopped to stare at him. "An alley off Wormwood? That's dueced specific," said Roger.

"There are murders all over London every day. Someone in particular you're wondering about?" Gus pinned Ben with a stare.

"Remember Mr. Felton, the night watchman?" asked Ben.

Gus and Clayton nodded.

Roger shrugged. "Didn't you mention something about his wife? She's a knocker-up?"

"Yes, well, she's his daughter, and she thinks she witnessed a murder yesterday morning."

"She thinks?" Clayton raised a brow.

Ben described the scene and the possible murderer. "No shots sounded, but she saw a knife in his hand."

Roger let out a whistle. "Doesn't sound good. He's likely floating, and we won't see him for a while."

"Rooney wasn't around today, but no one mentioned it. He was one of the men who wanted out." Clayton stopped talking as Bess came in with plates on her arm and a jug of ale.

When she set a plate before Gus, he gave her a side-glance and mumbled, "Thank ye, Bess."

The girl's face lit up, and she self-consciously pushed a brown curl beneath her mobcap. "Yer welcome." She refilled the men's bumpers and left.

Clayton began again, "Describe the man."

Ben did as asked.

"The devil if that doesn't sound like Rowland. Got that scar as a boy in his first fight. Acts like a rooster, parading around with his chest puffed out, wanting to lead the wolf pack. Says the ones left are spineless, and he'll make 'em into men."

"Do you think he got rid of Rooney?" asked Gus.

"Wouldn't surprise me." Clayton chewed on a hunk of bread. "He may be trying to impress The Vicar. He's a hobbledehoy—guessing about eighteen, maybe twenty. Arrogant enough to think he's got the experience to move up with a few misdeeds, and young enough to end up in the Thames himself."

"I ain't heard anything on Bow Street," said Roger, proud of his new position. "I'll keep my ears peeled."

"A Peeler keeping his ears peeled," barked Clayton. "Good one, except I believe the correct phrase is keep your eyes peeled."

Roger groaned and rolled his eyes.

"Would this Rowlands try to find Miss Felton?" asked Ben, his nerves taut at the thought of that sweet lass in the path of The Vicar.

"He's arrogant, not stupid. Yes, if he can find her, he'll silence her. The bloody cull has no conscience." Clayton studied Ben. "Are you worried for her, Ben?"

"I-I like her—and her father—and don't want to see either harmed."

"Maybe Sam could let her stay at Hospital Hope," offered Gus.

Ben mulled that over. "Possibility." Their brother Sam Brooks and his wife had opened a hospital for unwed mothers. The only option most of the unfortunate women had was to abandon their babes to a foundling home. The Magdalene House would take in repentant, wayward women, but they had to give up their children.

Roger shook his head. "Too many people there to identify her. No one can know where she is if she is to be truly safe."

"Can she sew?"

Ben frowned at Clayton. "I don't know. I assume so since she's... you know, a female."

Gus guffawed. "Don't let Maggie or Nora hear you say that. They made sure we can all darn a sock if needs be."

Embarrassment chased up Ben's neck. "I can ask her. Why?"

"Genie was talking about hiring an assistant. The business is growing, and she needs help. It wouldn't be hard to explain her presence."

Clayton's fiancée, along with her aunt, owned a dress and apparel shop on Clements Street. A random place to keep Miss Felton safe with no connection to her family or the murder. "Do you think Genie would mind a boarder for a week or so?"

"Let me talk to her. Find out if your girl has any skill with a needle," said Clayton. "Now, that particular lovely woman is waiting to plant a kiss on me as soon as I grace her doorway."

"Speakin' of arrogant," Roger whispered loudly.

Clayton only chuckled and hit the top of Roger's head with his cap. "Let me see what I can find out. I'm meeting up with a few of the congregation after midnight."

"Thank you," said Ben, hoping Clayton was wrong about the scarred man.

The night was warm for April, and he walked along Bush Lane toward Cannon Street. His mind was crowded with thoughts of Miss Felton, murder, and his new client, Lord Tamber. When he stopped for a moment, he realized he was on Walbrook Street. There was a light on at the Feltons', so before he overthought it, Ben knocked on the door.

Miss Felton called from the other side in a strange, husky tone. "Yeah?"

"It's Mr. Cooper," he said to the smooth wood, grinning at her attempt to disguise her feminine voice. "If you harm a hair on Miss Felton's head, it will be your last act on this earth."

The door swung open, and a brilliant smile took his breath away. He couldn't name the exact feeling every time he saw this girl, but it was overwhelming and wonderful at the same time.

"Oh, Miss Felton," he said in feigned surprise.

"You knew it was me," she said, standing back to let him enter. "I appreciate the gesture, though."

Ben walked to the table and stood by the chair he'd occupied that morning. Spread across the table were scraps of a variety of materials, along with buttons, shiny things, paste jewels, and lace. There were several different sizes of needles sticking out of a red wool pincushion. The clutter answered one question.

When he turned to see the door still open, it hit him. "I apologize, miss," he stammered. "Propriety didn't occur to me. I was walking, and thinking, and then I saw I was on your street..."

She laughed, and he realized her hair was down, black curls spilling over her shoulders. His fingers itched to see if the tresses were as soft as they looked. "It's fine. I'll leave the door open, and Mr. Mercer will hear me scream if you're improper."

His eyes flew to the ceiling, as if the image of a

cackling old man would wave back at him. "I give you my word."

"Did you come with news?" Her voice held hope.

He nodded. "I'm afraid your father is correct. You may be in danger."

She swallowed, and his eyes lingered on her slender white neck peeking above the high pale-rose collar. Tears shone in her eyes, sending a bolt of pain straight to his heart.

"Don't cry," he said, feeling helpless. If this was his sister, he'd wrap Nora in a tight hug. But she wasn't his sister. Far, far from being his sister.

"I have no place to go where I wouldn't put someone else in danger." Her bottom lip trembled just before the tears spilled over onto her cheeks. "I d-don't know what to do."

Ben watched her slim shoulders shake while her hands covered her face. He reached out to pat her arm, not sure how to comfort her, when he suddenly found himself holding her.

*How the devil did this happen?* he wondered as he rocked her back and forth, rubbing her back, his chin resting on her head. Her hair smelled of lemon and something flowery, and he breathed in the scent. Her dark waves shone in the lamplight, and beneath his palm, he found the tresses comparable to fine silk.

Just as suddenly, she pushed away, shaking her head. "Now I must apologize," she said, a look of horror in her shimmering eyes. "I don't know what came over me."

"Fear," he said softly. "A human emotion which

usually requires some means of comfort." He wanted to lighten the mood, take her mind off the grim situation.

His hands reached out to cup her face, wiping the tears away with his thumbs. Before his brain could refuse, his lips brushed her cheek, then lingered... His body's reaction to the contact was immediate. A desire of such intensity surged through him that it almost knocked the breath from his chest. But it wasn't just a physical desire, a man wanting a woman. It was a longing to protect her, to make her happy, to have her smile light up his world every day for the rest of his life.

Miss Felton peered up at him and sniffled, confusion clouding her deep-violet eyes. "Th-thank you for being so k-kind and helping me."

*Blast!* It was as if some other man had taken control, pushing Ben forward to seize the moment.

Her cheeks were splotchy from crying, her sooty lashes spiked from the tears. He'd never seen her look more beautiful. He ached to pull her back into his arms and swear to her that no one would ever hurt her. That he would keep her safe till his dying breath.

*Perdition!* What kind of tricks was his mind playing on him?

He could hear Maggie's words in the back of his brain as she scolded one of his brothers.

*It's not yer brain, ye daft man. It's yer heart.*

# CHAPTER 8

*Next afternoon*

Kitty forced a smile on her face as her father stared at her. Mr. Cooper was explaining the possible danger to their family and a plan to keep them all from peril.

"There was no murder reported and no body found," continued the solicitor. "But there is someone missing in the gang my brother has infiltrated. Someone who wanted out. The new arch rogue fits Miss Felton's description, and he's been trying to work his way up the ladder, so to speak."

Kitty took a deep breath. If Mr. Cooper thought this was best, she would do it. Her brain told her he was an intelligent man and a caring one. Her heart said she could trust him. And her body... Well, after last night, her body wanted to stay close too. She'd never experienced the feelings that fluttered through her each time she saw him.

"Unfortunately, I cannot tell you where your daughter will be. It would no longer be a safe house if—"

"Do you think I would give out information on the whereabouts of my Kitty?" bellowed her father. "I'd let them beat me to death before I said a word."

"Pa, that's not what he means." She ran to his side and pulled on his arm, making him look at her. "You're a terrible liar, and your temper is short when it comes to anyone threatening those you love."

"As soon as we can apprehend this man, Kitty may return, and you can both resume your lives in peace." Ben swiped a hand over his head, forcing strands between his fingers.

Kitty fisted her hands. She wanted to smooth the tufts back down. *Stop.* Her life was in danger, and she's thinking of playing with a man's hair.

"When will you… take her?" Her father's tone broke her heart.

"What shall I bring?" she asked. "How much should I pack?"

"Bring whatever occupies you in the evenings. Try to keep something normal in your daily schedule. I'm not sure how long. Clothes for at least a week?"

Kitty sensed a false optimism in Mr. Cooper's tone. It might be longer. "Will you escort me?"

"I'm afraid not. I am one of your customers, and I know your father. It will be my older brother." He smiled for the first time. "Sir Harry Walters can don a disguise, and Paddy himself wouldn't recognize him. He will pick you up and take you to a nearby public house, where you will walk straight out the back door. A hackney will be waiting to take you to your temporary home."

"Sir Harry?" Kitty recognized the shock in her voice. "I thought all of your siblings came from humble beginnings?"

"We did. It's a story for another time." Mr. Cooper took a sip of his tea, presumably giving her and Pa a moment to digest all this information.

"Will I… Will I be alone?" She imagined a dark room somewhere, biding the time with books, her piece work, and too much imagination. It would be the longest week of her life.

"We'll send Terry with you," her father said quickly.

"No, no," intervened Mr. Cooper, "you won't be alone. I can only say I think you will get on well with your hosts. And we'd trust them with our own lives."

It was decided Mr. Walters would arrive the next morning. She would miss Sunday service. Hot tears burned the back of her eyes, but she refused to shed them. This man was doing his best, and she would not cause him additional concern. Or add more stress on her father. If only she could bring Terry.

But Mr. Cooper was right. The terrier might be more recognizable than she was.

*SUNDAY MORNING*

Her traveling bag was packed, and her basket for her accessories sat by the door. She rocked back and forth, breathing deeply, thinking of her mother. Was Mama watching over her now?

The knock came too soon, and her father growled at the sound as he opened the door.

"Good morn," croaked the old man. "The Felton residence, I presume?"

Pa nodded to the man and granted him entrance.

Sir Harry Walters was a man of medium height and serious, dark-brown eyes. He wore a worn but presentable beaver hat and a black great coat in the same condition. His boots were dusty, along with the wooden cane he now leaned on. His gray hair was tied back at the neck, emphasizing his pale skin. Spectacles perched on the tip of his nose, and when he smiled, it appeared two of his teeth were missing. He leaned on a wooden cane with a black handle.

Her father gazed at the man in disbelief. "You're the man who will protect my daughter?"

Mr. Walters stood straight, his voice changing from crackling and aged to deep, vibrant, and confident.

"Yes, sir, I am. Excuse the costume, but we thought it best." He held out his hand to shake her father's. An obviously strong grip.

"I see," murmured Pa, still studying the man. "Will I at least get word somehow?"

"Aye," said Walters, "through me or Cooper."

Kitty crouched and scratched Terry's ears, then picked him up and hugged him. "I will miss you, my sweet pup. Don't forget me and take care of Pa." He licked her face, his tail creating a small breeze as it flapped back and forth.

Then she hugged her father, squeezing him with all her might. "I love you, Pa. Please try not to worry too much."

"I would take your place if I could. You know that, don't you?" he asked, holding her face gently in his big hands and kissing her forehead. "We'll be together again before you know it."

She nodded, pasted on a smile, and turned to Sir Harry. To her surprise, he opened his great coat and untied what looked to be a black ribbon wrapped around his waist. He looped it onto the handle of her traveling bag, made a tight bow, then closed his coat. As he resumed his bent posture, it was barely noticeable.

"Can't have it look like you're going anywhere for long, eh?" he said with a wink, the aged voice returning. "The basket is often used for shopping, so that can stay visible."

Kitty saw the approval in her father's eyes, the relief knowing Mr. Walters was indeed good at what he did. She had on her mother's cloak with the hood pulled low, not wanting to don the one she'd worn on the day of the murder.

"If we're stopped for any reason, your name is Alice," Mr. Walters said in his reedy tone. "Shall we?" He held out an elbow.

Kitty gathered all her courage, a last glimpse around her beloved home, and nodded. They walked out the door, and she refused to look back. The sight of her father and her dog watching her walk away would be more than she could bear.

She and the old man went two blocks before turning right, then another right turn onto Queen Street. They seemed to be going in a circle. The streets were fairly busy with vendors and shoppers, but no one noticed an old man with a young woman. They had to pause twice for carriages and wagons to pass as they crossed the road. When they reached Watling, Sir Harry stopped at the Clatterly Public House.

"I came here once with my parents," she said as they entered.

The barkeep was an older man with a round belly, dark eyes, and a bald pate—except for a few tufts of gray hair around his ears. He and Mr. Walters exchanged a nod, but they kept walking toward the back of the room. In the kitchen was an older, plump lady, her brown hair streaked with silver. Her smiling brown eyes locked with Kitty's, then she too nodded at Kitty's escort. They passed a little girl, maybe six or seven, washing pots. She paused to push a blonde lock from her big brown eyes and smiled at them. Kitty smiled back, wondering if she was the owner's granddaughter.

Leaving through the back as Mr. Cooper had described, Mr. Walters opened the door of a waiting hackney and assisted her in. Without any instructions to the driver, he joined her inside, sitting across from her.

"This will be a very short ride."

She nodded, lifting a slat on the shuttered windows

to see their progress. The coach turned onto Cheapside Street, then Lombard. Finally, they went right onto Clements Street and stopped in an alley across from St. Clement Church.

"I'm hiding in the open?" she asked, realizing with relief that she was still within her own neighborhood.

Mr. Walters grinned. "I always say keep it simple. You know where we're at?"

"Of course, I've passed this lane often. Am I to stay at the church?" She imagined a rector could be sworn to secrecy.

He laughed, a deep, warm sound. Kitty decided she liked this "old man" and wondered if she'd recognize him if she saw him again.

"You will be staying at Madame Chapelle's shop. She's a modiste—"

"She's brilliant! I've seen her work," gushed Kitty, temporarily forgetting the gravity of her situation. "I will live in her shop?" How would that work? Hide in the backroom?

Another rumble from Mr. Walters, his dark eyes twinkling. "We've arranged for a proper bed, miss. Genie, er, Miss Chapelle has made it known she is hiring an assistant due to the growth of her business. If anyone catches a glimpse of you, she will tell them you are her new employee."

Kitty closed her eyes for a brief moment. A dream come true if she *was* the assistant. Perhaps…

"I will also insist your hair be tucked up under a cap of some type. The midnight color is lovely but too easily remembered." He rose in a crouch and opened the door, peeking out. "Wait here, and I'll make sure the door is unlocked, and they are ready for you."

When Mr. Walters returned, he opened the carriage door, which blocked any view from the street, and escorted her into the building. To the right was a staircase, and in front of them a short hallway, leading to a door that she assumed was the modiste's shop. Mr. Walters led her up the stairs and knocked on the door.

It was answered by an older woman with frizzy light-brown hair and brown eyes that sparkled with bits of gold. "Here you are," she said with a bright smile. "Welcome, Miss Felton."

Behind her was Miss Eugenia Chapelle, whose reputation for excellence at a fair price had put her in high demand by the residents of Cheapside. She was younger than Kitty had expected, slender and beautiful, with the same eyes as the older woman—mother, perhaps?—and shiny wheat-blonde hair.

"This is Mrs. Peckton," said Mr. Walters, indicating the woman who'd answered the door. "She is part-owner of the business downstairs. And this is her niece and the modiste, Miss Chapelle."

Kitty, in awe and not knowing how to behave in this absurd circumstance, gave them both a quick curtsy. "I'm so grateful to you both for taking me in."

"Nonsense, and don't do that again. We're all of the same class here," said Mrs. Peckton. "Mrs. O'Brien is a close friend of mine, and we're happy to help any way we can."

"Of course we are," added Miss Chapelle. "We didn't hesitate when Clayton asked."

Kitty looked to Mr. Walters, not knowing who Clayton was. "My brother, Clayton Pierce."

"Soon to be my husband," said Miss Chapelle with a grin. "Would you like some tea, Harry?"

"I wish I had the time," he said, taking Kitty's traveling bag from beneath his great coat. Then he removed his spectacles and the wig, rubbing his short, almost-black hair.

Kitty noticed gray already coloring the tips and accentuating the temples. She also realized he was a striking man. Were all of Mr. Cooper's brothers so good-looking?

"Mattie will skin me alive if I'm late for our walk with her brother and mother," he said, nodding to each woman as he backed toward the door. "I'll be checking on you, Miss Felton. If you need anything at all, let these lovely ladies know, and I'll have it sent right away."

"A small portion of sanity, perhaps?" Kitty asked, trying to lighten the awkward moment.

"I'll take some of that too," said Miss Chapelle with a smirk. "Aunt Lydia?"

Mrs. Peckton laughed. "I gave up being sane years ago. It's not as necessary as one might think."

Kitty was shown to a small room, tastefully decorated with lavender rugs, a matching counterpane, and drapes. The wallpaper had lavender sprigs painted in rows against a cream background, as did the fireplace curtain. There was a wardrobe with one door open, showing half of the space empty.

"We weren't sure how much you would bring or

how long you would stay. So I moved some of my things into Genie's, where I'll share her room." Mrs. Peckton set Kitty's bag on the top of the bed.

"Oh, no. I don't want to take your space." Kitty was grateful but horrified to put someone out of their own room.

"Nonsense. Besides, the other bed is bigger and will fit us both fine. Make yourself comfortable, then join us in the kitchen for tea." Mrs. Peckton squeezed Kitty's shoulder. "Everything will be fine, my dear. No one better to take care of you than Maggie's boys."

When the door was closed, Kitty sank onto the soft tick and let herself go. The tears came slowly at first, then increased with intensity. She kept her sobs quiet, so as not to worry her kind hosts. How would her father fare without her? Had Terry tried to follow them? What would Pa tell her brother Joe when she didn't arrive for dinner tonight? She missed them already.

Kitty needed to freshen her appearance after that cleansing cry. Peering into the white glazed pitcher on the dressing table, she saw there was water inside. She poured some into the matching wash basin, then splashed her face, and patted her skin dry with the cotton towel lying next to the basin. With a corner of the cloth soaked in the cold water, she applied it to her eyes for a few minutes, hoping they wouldn't be so red-rimmed when she joined the other ladies.

Kitty took her spare dress, shift, and stockings from her traveling bag and put them away in the wardrobe, along with her pelisse. She closed her eyes and thought of her mother.

*Think of it as an adventure,* she always said when Kitty was nervous about trying something new.

Yes, that is how she would consider this. An adventure or holiday. And she had two new friends waiting to greet her.

# CHAPTER 9

*Next morning*
*Madame Chapelle's, Clements Street*

Kitty finished drying the dishes from breakfast, then fetched her basket. She spread the contents on the large wooden table and sat down, studying the bits and pieces. What would she create today? She had brought along several swaths of different material for reticules. Choosing the cinnamon shade, she poked a finger in the pouch of piping and chose two lengths of black, then studied the sequins. Embroidery or gewgaws?

Her mind wandered to her hosts. They were so kind, both insisting she call them by their given name so she would feel more of a friend and guest rather than a runaway. Over an evening of whist and interesting patter, she learned Genie had inherited her half of the shop from her mother. The poor woman, unwed and pregnant, had fled to London from a country estate when her father, the estate steward, had cast her out.

Pretending to be the widow of a French count, she had taken the moniker Madame Chapelle, providing a decent living for herself and her growing daughter. When Mrs. Peckton's husband died, she had joined her sister and niece, helping with the shop and the rent. Kitty was in awe of how the women had grown the business on their own. Genie seemed so happy with her success and upcoming marriage.

*Will I ever be as happy? Will I find success and love? At least one of the two?* And if she had to choose one, which would it be? Success or love? But she already knew the answer, thinking of her parents. Love would provide her with a better life than success, wouldn't it?

She could see the top of St. Clement Church from the kitchen window. Soon she was quietly singing the nursery rhyme.

*Oranges and lemons, say the bells of St Clement's.*
*You owe me five farthings, say the bells of St. Martin's.*
*When will you pay me, say the bells at Old Bailey.*
*When I grow rich, say the bells at Shoreditch.*
*When will that be, say the bells of Stepney.*
*I do not know, say the great bell of Bow.*
*Here comes a candle to light you to bed,*
*And here comes a chopper to chop off your head!*
*Chip chop, chip chop, the last man is dead.*

. . .

THERE WAS a public dispute about the origin of the lyrics. This smaller church insisted its location, close to the docks where citrus fruit was unloaded, proved it was the church in the rhyme. But St. Clement Danes Church of Westminster proclaimed it is the St. Clement's featured in the children's poem.

"What do we have here?" asked Genie, chuckling when she startled Kitty. "I'm sorry. I didn't mean to startle you."

The modiste wore an azure muslin with a square neckline and short, puffed sleeves. Tiny loops of white lace had been added to the collar and cuffs, and small doves were embroidered along the hem. A gown too lovely for Kitty to ever wear as a day dress. She suddenly felt like a bumpkin in her serviceable brown wool.

"It's my fault. My mind was wandering," Kitty said as she tried to scoop up the scattered tassels, beads, and materials scattered across the table.

"Don't stop. You've piqued my interest." Miss Chapelle sat across from her, her elbows planted on the surface as she stared at the reticule Kitty was working on. "Is this for you or someone else?"

"I-I... both. I buy scraps from seamstresses, bits and pieces that aren't enough to use for a project, so they're cheap. I know so many women who can't afford to replace their accessories. In this way, their old items can look and feel like new." She showed Genie a pair of gloves she'd finished for a customer. "The fingers were in good shape, but the cuff was frayed and dirtied. I cut it off and added a new one in a slightly different color, piping to cover the seam, then embroidered her initials in the same color."

Genie took the cotton glove and studied it. "Excellent work," she murmured. "I sell items like this. One-of-a-kind accessories to go with my gowns and pelisses. But it's so time-consuming. Any experience as a seamstress?"

"I learned from my mother, though I prefer this type of handiwork," admitted Kitty, her stomach churning with nerves. Was Madame Chapelle considering her as an employee? She might swoon. *Deep breath, deep breath.*

"I'm looking for an assistant to help with sewing." Genie tapped her mouth with a forefinger, the gold of her brown eyes bright as she considered. "Are you in need of work?"

Kitty's first instinct, because of her present "business venture," was to say no. But was spitting dried peas at someone's window the way she wanted to earn a living the rest of her life? Of course not. It was a way to earn coin to help her father. This—her eyes scanned the contents of her basket—was what she longed to do.

"Yes, I am," she said with conviction.

Genie smiled, showing straight white teeth. "I'll send Aunt Lydia up with something. We'll start with some hemming and check your stitches. If you are competent with what I need in an assistant, I'll hire you. Then we'll discuss the accessories and see what we can work out."

Kitty blinked as her mouth gaped. She swallowed, ignoring her pounding heart. "That would be fine," was all she managed to say without her voice sounding shrill.

When Miss Chapelle left, Kitty fell back against the hard wooden chair. An employee of Madame Chapelle's? She was confident in her sewing skills, even if it wasn't her passion.

*Mama, I wish you were here.*

Shortly after, a knock interrupted her thoughts. Why would Mrs. Peckton knock? *If her hands were full, nick ninny!* Kitty leapt to the door, tossed it open, then gasped.

"Mr. Cooper," she said in shock.

"Yes, that's me," he said, standing on the top step of the front staircase that led directly to the shop.

Her mouth was open again, so she quickly shut it. "I-I thought you were Mrs. Peckton."

He grinned, and she noted his blond hair was smoothed back, no spikes to be seen. "I am definitely not an elderly widow."

"Did he say elderly?" demanded the woman in question, coming up behind Mr. Cooper.

"No." Mr. Cooper's eyes widened in shock.

"Yes," Kitty said at the same time. He tossed her a glance of mock outrage when she disagreed with him. Kitty smirked at the blush creeping up his neck. "Oh, my manners." She stepped aside so he and Mrs. Peckton could enter.

Mr. Cooper hung his hat on a wall hook, then walked into the kitchen as if he was familiar with the apartment. Kitty followed behind the older—but *not* elderly—woman, carrying a heavy cerulean-blue velvet gown.

"I've brought a project for you," said Mrs. Peckton. "I've already torn out the hem and indicated the new length. I have needles and thread, so you won't need to use your own. I assume you have your own thimble?"

Kitty nodded. "Yes, ma'am. Thank you so much for this opportunity."

"Let's save the gratitude until we see your stitches," she said, all business. "I thought I'd observe your sewing a bit and peruse your crafts while I"—she gave Mr. Cooper a side-glance—"watch."

"Chaperone, you mean?" asked Mr. Cooper with a smirk. "Shall I make some tea?"

"You speak with your lady, and I'll make the tea."

Kitty's eyes grew wide at the term "your lady," and she looked at Mr. Cooper, whose flush had spread to his cheeks.

"I'm not his— "

"I just wanted to check on you, see how you were faring in your new surroundings."

His smile made the wings flutter in her belly. Perhaps he would visit more while she was here. That would be a bright spot in a cloudy sky. Kitty wanted to know him better.

"Miss Chapelle and Mrs. Peckton have been more than kind." She picked up the velvet gown and inspected the pulled hem, spreading it out on the table to snip off the frayed edge.

"Thank you again, ma'am," he said. "Clayton

mentioned this solution, but I didn't want to put anyone out."

"No thanks needed. You may have found us a new assistant," said Mrs. Peckton, joining them again at the table while the water heated on the coal stove. "We might owe you a favor."

"I'd say we're even if it works out," agreed Mr. Cooper, his eyes never leaving Kitty as she threaded a needle with dyed thread, then began measuring the hem according to the mark.

As she worked, Kitty told Mrs. Peckton about her hope of making accessories to earn a living. The woman inspected her work and nodded her approval.

"The accessories can be almost as time-consuming as the gowns. Poor Genie can barely keep up with those orders, let alone the accompanying bonnets, reticules, gloves… I really hope you are able to help her."

Kitty swallowed, pushing back the thrill at the idea of her dream becoming reality. Her eyes strayed to Mr. Cooper, the reason she was here. "I think you are my lucky charm."

"Me? Lucky?" He chortled, a lopsided grin on his face. "Luck has never been my friend. I've been teased about my lack of it since I was a boy. My sister Nora says I was born under a halfpenny planet."

"I don't believe that," said Kitty. "You are a solicitor with an excellent reputation. Your family is well-liked and respected. Of course you are lucky."

"I have never won a game of chance in my life," he said emphatically. "No one will take me on as a partner in a card game or even charades. I always lose when betting on a horse—or anything else for that matter."

"He speaks the truth," said Mrs. Peckton, an amused smile crinkling the corners of her brown eyes.

"Never?" asked Kitty, unconvinced.

He shook his head. "Marbles? Torture. Always put in impossible situations and lost. My brothers could sneak into the kitchen and steal a last piece of pie or a biscuit, but I was caught every time."

"That doesn't necessarily mean you are luckless," argued Kitty, imagining him as an adorable little boy with yellow hair sticking up in a dozen directions. "Your skills are in other areas."

"If there were three or four of us waiting to cross a street, and a carriage passed by, I would be the only one to get splashed. If I tried to beat the rain, I would be drenched every time." He waved Mrs. Peckton to stay seated as he walked to the stove and removed the boiling water.

Kitty cut another length of thread and rethreaded her needle.

"It became known in the household that if I was brought along, anything bad would happen to me instead of them. I became a sort of insurance for my siblings." Mr. Cooper chuckled. "Harry and Gus would take me to St. James's Park, and we'd watch the cavalry practice. Sometimes the men would race each other, and bets were made. Before placing a bet, my brothers would ask me which horse I chose. They made sure to take any other."

"So you were a lucky piece, er, person, for them?" Kitty laughed at his story. "You've proved my point."

"Maggie says his luck flies the coop and lands on others," said Mrs. Peckton.

"And I am the latest happy recipient." Kitty looked up at Mrs. Peckton, who was studying the stitches she'd made so far. "Smaller?" she asked.

"No, those are perfect. Genie will be pleased." She walked to a cupboard and took out four teacups, saucers, and spoons, setting them on a tray already laden with a small silver bowl. A large lump of sugar rested on the counter. She broke off a half-dozen chunks and placed them in a bowl. "Do you take milk?"

"No, ma'am," said Kitty, quickly collecting her items from the table and returning them to the basket to make room for the tea tray. She noted Mrs. Peckton already knew how Mr. Cooper drank his since the tray did not have milk.

An hour later, after more tales of woe from the solicitor and two cups of tea, Mrs. Peckton squinted at Kitty's stitches again. "Yes, you might be just what we need." She turned to Mr. Cooper. "I am going downstairs now. We have a client coming at half past one. I expect to see you close behind me, Benjamin."

*Benjamin.* What a wonderful and solid name. Possibly *Ben* to his family and friends? Kitty laid the gown on the table and stood too. She would follow them to the door and bid Mr. Cooper farewell. There would be no hint of impropriety. She would not chance offending these generous women.

Seeing Kitty stand, Mr. Cooper rose with a

martyred sigh. "I suppose I need to return to my office and finish going over some documents. May I stop in again, Miss Felton? To, uh, see how you fare?"

She almost giggled. "It is not my home. You will need to ask Mrs. Peckton or Miss Chapelle." Oh, but she wanted him to come again.

"Genie and Lydia," reprimanded the older woman over her shoulder.

"I shall let your father know all is well when he wakes me tomorrow," he said, turning to face her as Mrs. Peckton made her way down the narrow steps. "Would you like that?"

"I would be ever so grateful." Kitty locked her gaze with his whiskey-colored eyes, heat rushing to her core. His head lowered just an inch or so, and she thought he would... *Don't be a ninny. Why would he kiss me?*

"Would you mind if I asked him permission to court you?" he asked in a husky whisper.

She swallowed, not sure if she'd heard him correctly over her thumping heart. "What?"

"Miss Felton, it would be my honor if I could see more of you. Not as a protector." His eyes darkened like brandy, roaming her face, landing on her lips.

The heartbeat seemed to vibrate through her body, and she resisted the urge to wipe her palms against her skirt. She nodded, not able to form any words. When he leaned toward her, her eyes grew wide, then slammed closed. His mouth covered hers, moving back and forth gently. A thrumming began in her lower belly. Her knees wobbled. Her fingers clutched his lapels, fearing she would sink, drowning in the feel of his soft lips against hers.

Kitty wasn't sure what that new emotion was rushing through her. It was like a sudden summer storm. Unexpected and exciting.

He pulled back, leaving her panting. When she opened her eyes, he wasn't smiling. He lifted his hand and pushed a lock of her hair from her cheek with his knuckle. It was a simple yet provocative gesture. *Oh my.* This man would be trouble for her.

Breathtaking, astonishing, irresistible trouble.

# CHAPTER 10

*Next day*
*Chancery Lane, London*

"You'll have to come to the club for a drink sometime," said Lord Tamber, placing his beaver hat firmly on his dark head. "I can introduce you to some friends."

"I'd like that very much, my lord," said Ben. "If you have any other questions, don't hesitate to contact me."

"I'm not a hesitating kind of man," he said with a chuckle. "My brother and I were taught to go after what we wanted."

Ben knew most titled men were raised in the same fashion, encouraged to take whatever they desired and to the devil with everyone else. Ben liked the earl, though, who was more approachable than most noblemen he was acquainted with. Then he remembered Harry's brother-in-law, the Earl of Darby. A man with integrity and a lack of class prejudice. Perhaps it just depended on the man, like the rest of the human race.

It was after five, and he was meeting Clayton at the Stock Exchange Coffee House for a drink and a meal. He hoped to find Mr. Felton on his nightly rounds afterwards, let him know his daughter was safe, and ask permission to court her. He clenched his teeth, hating the nerves that overtook him whenever he thought of it. *Why?* He'd never been anxious before when it came to women.

His last courtship had been with a young widow. A prime article, blonde with sea-green eyes and a delightful laugh. But she hadn't been interested in a relationship, enjoying the freedom widowhood had brought her. That had been a year ago, and no one had caught his attention until Miss Felton. *Kitty.* Oh, how he longed to make her purr. Hold her in his arms, kiss those soft lips again, whisper in her ear and feel her shiver.

*I'm getting ahead of myself,* he thought as he stepped out onto busy Chancery Lane. The street was filled with vehicles, people trying to cross between the carriages and wagons, crowds moving both ways on each side of the street. A man bumped into him, mumbled an apology, and continued on. A scraggly dog dashed under a carriage, spooked the horses, and barely escaped a crushing wheel.

Most of the vendors were closing up, their wares sold by now. He increased his pace, knowing he had an hour's walk, but enjoying the warmer weather too much to wave a hackney.

Would Clayton have good news? Ben desperately wanted the murderer to be found, so he could begin courting her in earnest. Living with strangers in fear for your life and your family was not the proper way to begin a relationship. He wanted her to come to know him, the man, not the solicitor whose family saved her. He was looking for, hoping for love not gratitude. In the present situation, he wouldn't be sure about the reason for her affection—*if* any affection grew between them.

*Weel, boyo, I t'ink ye've already let that cow out of da barn.*

Ben chuckled to himself, thinking of what Paddy might say. His folks had an Irish saying for every situation. He thought of Miss Felton and her courage, and the tears she held back when speaking of her father and her dog.

He snapped his fingers. That's what he'd do. Yes, she would like that. Ben decided to ask Paddy the next day. But first, he had to speak to a father about his daughter.

THE COFFEE HOUSE was humming with customers. It was a popular public house for bankers and neighborhood businessmen. It was close to home for both him and Clayton, who lived on Threadneedle. For now. Ben wondered how long before Clayton and Genie would purchase a townhouse and move from his rooms. Clayton's place wasn't ideal for a family, and he had the impression the couple was eager to start one.

He nodded to Sally, the buxom barmaid who knew everyone's drink and favorite dish, and scanned the large room for his brother. Sally stopped in front of him, a tray filled with bumpers of ale and a half loaf of fresh bread.

"He's back there," she said with a toss of blonde curls. "Got some tasty rabbit stew today."

"Sounds perfect," he said with a wink, heading toward his brother who sat at the end of a long table.

"Brother, how goes the office?" Clayton asked with a snicker. "I don't know how you can sit behind a desk. I'd be dicked in the knob if I had to stay locked up in a room all day."

"First, I'm not locked in. I enjoy my work. It's not a prison. And I don't have to wear grimy clothes and forget what dialect I'm speaking on any given day."

"Point for Ben." Clayton nodded at the ale he had waiting for his brother. "Did you order the stew?"

"I usually take whatever Sally suggests. She's never steered me wrong." Ben took a long pull on the ale.

"She knows her customers," agreed Clayton. "I used to think I didn't need a wife between Sally, Bess at Dog's Bone, and my landlady."

"Genie has convinced you otherwise."

"I believe fate convinced us both." He looked over Ben's shoulder. "Here comes our girl."

Sally set down their bowls of steaming gravy,

vegetables, and meat, with a fresh hunk of bread and churned butter.

"If I wasn't betrothed, Sally..." Clayton grinned at her as he picked up a spoon.

"Before ye was betrothed, ye used to say, 'If I was a marryin' man.'" She rolled her eyes good-naturedly. "Anythin' else?"

"Everything I need," Ben said around a mouthful of potato, and Clayton echoed the sentiment.

When she had moved on, Clayton leaned forward. "I've put someone on Rowlands, hoping to catch him when he goes after the second man who wanted out. I'd almost feel sorry for the old gallows bird, but he wears the same feathers as Rowland."

"So you hope to catch him in the act?" Ben liked the idea, possibly eliminating the need for Miss Felton to testify. One murder would send the man to the gallows as easily as two.

"My main concern as we approach this is to keep my anonymity. I don't want to jeopardize my placement within The Vicar's gang." Clayton dug into his stew, emitting an appreciative groan. "I need to find a cook when we move to a bigger home. Genie's too busy to keep up a household, and we'll be losing her Aunt Lydia. That woman can make a pudding better than—"

"Don't say it!" Ben raised a hand. "Maggie'll find out somehow, and you will pay dearly."

Clayton snorted. "You're right. But it's true."

"I'm surprised Rowlands hasn't already taken the other man out."

"Like I said, he's a coxcomb to be sure, but he's also a fox. He told us last night he had no idea what happened to the man, but he wished him well. Then laughed." Clayton waved his empty bumper in the air and smiled, presumably catching Sally's eye. "I need to be careful not to arouse his suspicions. Rowland's got skill at spreading flim flam and luring natty lads into the fold. He's brought in four new recruits in the last couple of weeks."

"I'm sure it takes a certain degree of finesse to do that. He's offering them a job they can never walk away from." How many wayward lads had fallen in with the wrong people? It was an age-old tale.

"The typical ruse. Street urchins are used to being on the wrong side of the law, so they snatch up the generous wage for something they'd be doing anyway. Once they're comfortable, they're asked to do something a little more dangerous—and more pay."

"Locked in before they know it's happened."

"Exactly. I imagine Rowlands himself learned the trick the hard way."

"Are you concerned for your safety?" Ben worried about his brothers, putting themselves in danger for most cases, though he knew how much they loved their work. And they were deuced good at it. Ben appreciated the information he learned as a Runner, knowing what was needed for a case before it could be presented at court and how much work it took to attain that information.

He didn't enjoy the violence. He would fight, if needed, and rather enjoyed a good boxing match. His marksmanship was excellent, and he would shoot another man to preserve his life or someone else's, but he much preferred assisting through his practice.

"I'm always concerned about safety—mine and any innocent victims—but it's part of the job." He paused while Sally refilled their bumpers. "I'm thankful Genie has never asked me to quit. She understands how important the cases are to me."

"You've found a good woman. I'm glad you didn't make a bumblebath of the whole relationship and let Harry talk some sense into you." Ben remembered how Clayton had almost lost Genie. She made him a better man.

*Is that what I want? To be a better man?* Then he was about to court the right woman because he was certain Miss Felton would have the same effect on him.

"I put Lynch on surveillance for the Felton place at night," added Clayton, ignoring Ben's statement about the mess he almost made of his betrothal. "If Rowlands knows who the witness is, he'll show up at her residence when she's alone."

"I hadn't thought of that. If no one comes looking for her, then they haven't been able to discover her identity. She may be safe after all."

Hope bloomed in Ben's chest. While Kitty would still need to stay out of sight so she wasn't spotted, the issue of her safety would be greatly reduced. "Roger must not need much sleep. Doesn't he have regular hours now?"

"Paddy talked to his constable. He's helping us with

this case, and all information will be directly relayed to Bow Street."

"Smart." Ben took a deep breath, then set down his spoon.

"Uh-oh, whatever you're about to tell me must be serious." Clayton followed suit and gave Ben his full attention.

"I'm speaking with Mr. Felton. I want to court his daughter." There, he'd said it out loud. It hadn't been so bad.

Clayton let out a whistle. "She's a beauty. There must be something special about her to lure you out from under the rock you've been hiding under."

"I haven't been hiding. I just needed to re-establish my priorities, make a wise decision about my future."

"And find the right girl," said Clayton with a knowing wink. "Be as practical as you want, but it doesn't matter when Cupid strikes. All sense flies out the window."

"You should know," said Ben, raising his ale to toast his brother. "To the parson's trap."

"To tailormade leg-shackles," agreed Clayton.

* * *

BEN WALKED the neighborhood until he found Mr. Felton. He stepped in beside him after scratching Terry's ears.

"She's doing well," said Ben.

Mr. Felton nodded, unusually quiet. He probably missed his daughter.

"Someone is tailing the suspect, hoping to catch him when he goes after the next man."

"Good to hear," said the night watchman.

"A man will also be surveilling your place. My brother reasoned that, if no one comes looking for Miss Felton, the suspect doesn't know her identity." Ben saw the deep lines in the older man's face soften.

"This business needs to be over, so I can bring my Kitty home."

*Woof!*

Terry's agreement made both men chuckle, easing the tension. Ben plowed ahead, throwing subtlety to the wind.

"I'd like your permission to court your daughter." He was appalled at the relieved sigh that had forced its way out of his chest. And shocked at Mr. Felton's reaction.

"It took you long enough," he said, slapping Ben on the shoulder. "It's a good thing you're a solicitor and not a barrister. You wear your heart on your sleeve, son. Or in your eyes, at least."

Ben grinned. "I can't deny it. It's a fault I was born with."

"Not a fault, my boy. It makes it easier for people to know you speak the truth."

"Are you giving me your consent, then?" This had been too easy.

"I'm for it, but you'll have to convince Kitty. She has it in her head that a husband would keep her from doing the things she wants to do. She's dead set on making of business with her gewgaws."

"She's against marriage?" Ben asked, flabbergasted. Didn't all women want a husband and a family?

"No, nothing like that. She's just willing to wait for the right partner. You'll have to prove you're that man." Mr. Felton looked at Ben and let out a guffaw, slapping his knee. "You've turned as pale as the mornin' milk."

"I always thought women—"

"There's your first mistake. Don't try to rationalize a woman's actions, for their minds don't work the same as ours. You'll end up in Bedlam."

Ben began to laugh, and soon Mr. Felton joined him. "I wish you luck, my boy. Nothing I'd like more than to welcome you to the family."

Ben's smile crumpled. Luck? Oh nooooo.

# CHAPTER 11

*Two days later*
*Madame Chapelle's, Clements Lane*

Kitty popped the thread in her mouth, closed one eye, and threaded the needle. She was in the workroom of the shop, where she could easily access all the supplies necessary to complete her tasks. Life had taken such an unexpected turn.

In only a few days, she had witnessed a murder, been torn from her home, and become an employee of Madame Chapelle's. Genie and Lydia treated her like family, and she wanted nothing more than to do well by them. But she would prefer to sleep in her own bed. The workroom was bright with a large window facing the church across the street. The room itself was up a short flight of steps, so it wasn't at street level. Kitty could keep the curtains and window open without worry of a passerby spying her.

There was a long wooden table used for spreading out and cutting material. Several mannequins wore different orders in progress. Shelves across one wall held small bins of buttons, beads, threads, sequins, paste jewels—anything Kitty could imagine needing for her embellishments. She had proven to be fast and precise with a needle and would be paid according to the work finished.

Genie had decided to provide Kitty with a sketch the next time a client ordered an accessory to match a gown or pelisse. Kitty would be able to use Genie's own supplies but would work on the piece after shop hours. Lydia had suggested paying by the hour, having Kitty give them an estimate of the time needed to complete a project. They would add their profit to Kitty's estimate to figure the cost to the customer.

She would be under the aunt and niece's watchful eye to begin with. Kitty understood and had no qualms with that. Madame Chapelle's could open impossible doors for her. It already had with this new position as assistant. If only she could share her news with Pa and Joe. Hug Terry to her chest and feel his warm tongue tickling her cheek when he gave her a kiss.

Mr. Cooper would join them for supper tonight. Her breath caught as she thought of his handsome face, the kind, tawny eyes, and that devastating smile. She sighed, remembering their last goodbye. His warm lips against hers, his knuckles feathering her jaw. Her body craving more.

"Must be some fine thoughts running through that pretty head of yours," said Lydia Peckton, grinning at her. "I remember that expression well."

Kitty blushed and bent her head, trying to focus on the sleeve she was attaching to a jonquil spencer.

"Would it have to do with a certain Mr. Cooper?" she asked, her brows rising.

"It might," she admitted. When she looked up, Lydia's eyes sparkled with mischief.

"He's an excellent young man. Intelligent, kind, makes a good living, and handsome, though I suppose you haven't noticed the last."

Kitty snorted, then covered her nose with her hand, her eyes wide. Both women burst out laughing as Genie entered the room.

"What did I miss?" she asked, hands on her slim hips. She wore a lilac sprigged muslin, her hair pulled up in a loose chignon, long blonde curls falling against her cheeks. A simple lilac ribbon adorned her crown.

"Just teasing our new friend," said Lydia.

Those words warmed Kitty, and she blinked back the unexpected emotion. What generous hearts these ladies had, to admit her into their world without question and offer their friendship. If there were more people like them—and the O'Briens—the world would be a much sweeter place.

"Clayton told me a certain brother spoke with a certain person's father, giving said brother leave to court the daughter." This time, it was Genie waggling her brows.

"You would make a terrible spy," said Lydia, laughing. "In other words, we need to be sure to act as chaperones tonight when Benjamin arrives."

"I ordered the flounder from the fishmonger, and it will be delivered later this afternoon," Genie said, ignoring her aunt's jab. "I decided against the green hastens. I can't see spending the extra money on canned peas when they will be cheaper and fresh in July."

"I have early potatoes and some turnips left. I'm using the last of the carrots for a soup." Lydia leaned over Kitty's shoulder, observing the stitches.

Kitty was already used to the informal inspections and welcomed any advice for improvement. She had never been one to cringe from criticism, especially when it was well-intended. "Are the stitches close enough?"

"Up until here," said Lydia, pointing at a stitch that was a little off. "It won't take but a minute to pull those few out and redo it."

As she finished the sleeve, Kitty hummed. Since arriving, she had gone from devastated and frightened to optimistic about her future. The cards were falling in her favor. Perhaps Mr. Cooper *was* her lucky charm. Poor man, she thought with a grin.

*Cursed Cooper,* Mr. Walters had said. *At one point, we stopped using the term "with a little luck" because it never happened.*

Maybe she would turn out to be lucky for Cursed Cooper.

* * *

"THE FISH WAS PERFECT," said Mr. Cooper, wiping his mouth with a napkin. "According to my sister, Nora, flounder can be easy to overcook."

"That is correct, which is why it is better to poach it with lemon and a little white wine." Lydia beamed at the compliment. "I hope you saved room for dessert. I used the last of the winter pears to make a crumble."

"Be still, my heart," said Mr. Cooper.

When they gathered in the parlor, Genie took out a deck of cards, stared at it, then put it away. She gazed about the room, obviously searching for an activity that didn't include any type of luck.

Aunt Lydia came to the rescue. "Let's play a word association game. We will each have three slips of paper and will write a word on each. The first player chooses one from the bowl and announces the contents. Then each player afterwards must say a word that is associated."

Genie explained further, "So, I read the word 'sky,' the next player may say 'blue,' and the next says 'ocean' and so on?"

"Exactly," said Lydia. "There is no winner or loser, so *luck* has nothing to do with the game."

Kitty realized the ladies were trying to help Mr. Cooper save face from losing any games. It was typical of them to be so considerate, but she thought the solicitor was quite used to his lot. However, the game sounded intriguing, so she played along.

Genie passed around pencils and tore a sheet of paper into strips. They each wrote a word on the slips, folded them, and tossed them in a porcelain bowl.

Lydia picked up the container, stirred the paper with a forefinger, then chose a piece.

"Frog," she said with a laugh and turned to Kitty.

"Leg," Kitty said and looked at Mr. Cooper.

"Up," he quipped.

"Over," called out Genie.

"Spend," said Lydia.

"Thrift," added Kitty, smiling at Mr. Cooper.

"Maggie." He blinked, then roared with laughter.

Lydia smacked his knee. "Impertinent boy!"

They began again, and the evening flew by. Besides the word game, Lydia had shared some stories of when Genie was a girl. Genie shared that the stable-master at the local mews was sweet on Lydia. Mr. Cooper announced Nora had been cast in two Charles Macready performances at the Theatre Royal in June.

"Is it a major role?" asked Kitty, taking in the fact that his sister would be acting with the renowned Macready.

He shook his head. "No, but she's hoping by being in the production, she'll be noticed and considered for bigger parts."

"She's quite talented," said Lydia. "Voice of an angel."

"She can play almost any instrument," added Genie.

"Quite the paragon," murmured Kitty, already intimidated by the woman before even meeting her.

Mr. Cooper turned to her. "Would you like to see one of the plays?"

Her hand flew to her chest. "I'd love to. I've only seen the outdoor productions at Vauxhall when Mama was still alive. She would insist Pa take us once I was old enough."

"Hopefully, this situation will be resolved. Our family usually reserves a box when Nora performs, so it would be a family affair." He watched her, and she realized he was waiting to see her reaction.

She smiled. "That would be lovely. I look forward to meeting the rest of your family. Especially if they are anything like the members I'm already acquainted with."

When he made his farewells, Kitty rose to accompany him to the door.

"Why don't you see Benjamin down the stairs, dear," Lydia said to Kitty.

"Of course," she said, her heart soaring at the thought of a kiss to end a wonderful evening.

At the bottom of the stairs, she heard a click as someone shut the door above them. They were alone. Mr. Cooper turned to face her, holding his hat. He placed it on his head, freeing both hands to grip her waist and pull her closer.

"If I don't kiss you in the next minute, I will die," he whispered, his breath warm against her ear.

"We can't allow that," she said, tipping her face up. "I—"

His mouth claimed hers, stopping any further words or thoughts. It was only taste and touch. She breathed in his Bay Rum cologne, the spicy scent tickling her senses. His hands gripping her hips, sending an aching pulse low in her core as his hard body pressed against her.

She slipped her fingers around his neck, wondering how he knew just how to touch her, hold her, make her weak in the knees. When his tongue glided along the seam of her mouth, she parted her lips. When he entered her, she gasped against him, and soon he was holding her up, running a hand along her back.

When the kiss ended, her chest heaved as she tried to catch her breath and slow her thumping heart. They locked eyes, and the tenderness in those tawny orbs almost undid her. The thought flickered through her mind how easily an inexperienced girl could be seduced. Kitty would toss caution to the wind at this moment.

"Thank you," he said, his voice raw as he leaned his forehead against hers.

"For what?" She couldn't focus on words, her mind swirling with happiness and… passion? What was this tumultuous feeling flooding her body, her heart?

"For the kiss, for being you, for allowing me to—"

This time, it was Kitty who cut off the conversation with a kiss. Her arms went around his neck, knocking off his hat. His reaction was swift, turning her against the wall, his fingers running up her arms, down her waist. He let out a groan.

"If I don't leave now, we may both regret it," he rasped against her cheek.

"Never, Mr. Cooper." Feeling brave by his reaction, she tucked a finger in his cravat and pulled, placing her lips on his neck, just below his chin. His shiver had desire and power crashing within her chest.

"I believe Ben would be more appropriate at this

time," he murmured, placing a kiss on each eye, then her nose, and finally, finally her mouth again.

They both jerked back, ending the kiss at the sound of a key rattling in the upper door. "I'd wager that's a hint, *Ben*," she said, with a lazy smile. She liked the feel of his name on her lips.

"Kitty, when may I call on you again?" His voice pleaded with her, as if he was desperate to see her once more.

*Tomorrow at sunrise.*

"As soon as you can?" She would have no rest tonight. Her mind would be filled with dreams of a handsome, witty, intelligent man who kissed her breathless.

# CHAPTER 12

*One week later, early May*
*Gracechurch Street*

"Body found in the Thames this morning," announced Roger. "They're asking Sam to do the autopsy, so it stays quiet."

"Good. That means Clayton will have access and can identify him as one of the congregation or not." Paddy sat in the parlor in his usual chair by the fire, scratching Aonarach's back. The wolfhound's long neck arched up, his eyes closed as he enjoyed the rub.

"Have you seen anyone lurking around the Feltons?" asked Ben. Kitty was growing more homesick, desperate to see her family—and dog. He had an idea to help with that.

"Only once, two nights ago," said Roger. "But two drunks came stumbling down the lane and scared him off. Hasn't been back, so I don't know if it was a random thief or our man."

*Bollocks!* No playing the hero today.

"A few days ago, Rowlands was all cozy with one of the gang. I knew he was giving orders of some kind, but I couldn't hear. So I followed the man." Clayton leaned against the hearth, his elbow connecting with one of the frames on the mantel. He righted it before continuing, "It's happening soon. Rowlands has the man trailing the other member who wanted out."

"We know Rowlands committed the first murder, but he may have someone else take care of the other traitor," mused Paddy.

"Nah, he'll want the credit," disagreed Clayton.

Harry grunted. "Who shall we put on Rowlands?"

"Ye feel comfortable doin' it, Clayton? Or do you need to stay with the gang a wee longer? This could expose your identity." Paddy didn't like the undercover work, unable to help one of his boyos if something went wrong.

"I think it's best if I remain just another member. Something's brewing, and not a soul suspects me."

Paddy nodded. "Let's put Gus on the Felton place and send Lynch after Rowlands. How does that sound to everyone?" Due to his size, Gus was never used to tail anyone. It was one of the few things Gus couldn't do.

"Rowlands mentioned being summoned by The Vicar. He thinks he's getting a promotion," commented Clayton.

"You're not so sure?" asked Ben. Would Clay try to

accompany Rowlands to the meeting? The thought of his closest friend in the company of such a heinous villain sent a chill down his spine.

."Rowlands has never spoken with anyone higher than Mason. I can't see The Vicar trusting him enough to meet in person. I'm guessing he'll meet with a representative, or it may be a trap." Clayton pushed away from the fireplace. "Word may be out about Rowlands taking matters into his own hands. If The Vicar considers him a bomb ready to go off, sending any attention in his direction, Rowlands will be next."

"I agree. Da boss must be a wee bit on edge these days." Paddy stood, wincing a tiny bit when his knee popped. "I'll let Gus know where he's off to next. Keep me posted, boyos."

"Paddy," said Ben before they left. "Could I ask a favor?"

"Aye, whatcha need?"

"Kitty, er, Miss Felton is terribly homesick. I wanted to bring her pup to her for a visit, but I'm afraid it might make her, well—"

"Weepy?" asked Paddy with a grin.

"Yes. Do you mind if I brought Aonarach for a visit? I think it would be a nice distraction." Aonarach was like Paddy's grandson. If anything happened to the dog while he was in Ben's care… Well, he'd be moving to the Continent.

Paddy scratched his jaw. A sign he was considering it. "Did I tell you Nora was asking about your sweetheart?"

Ben's eyes widened. "No. I didn't even think she knew about Kitty."

Paddy barked a laugh. "Boyo, haven't ye learned anything living with those women? They *always* know when it comes to matters of the heart. Anyway, why don't I send Nora over tonight? I'll be making two of my children happy with one act."

"That would be excellent. Thanks, Paddy." He knew Kitty would love the big furry beast. Hopefully, Nora would bring back a good report to Maggie.

"Rumor has it ye're at Chapelle's most nights now." Paddy's large hand squeezed Ben's shoulders. "Ye're keen on dis lass, eh?"

"Yes, sir." *Blast! Don't blush.* "I hadn't realized how much I needed the company."

"Dat's what a good woman does to ye. I'm happy for ye. Her father's a good man. Ye could do worse, as my pater always said." Now he slapped Ben on the back. "I was wonderin' how long it would take ye to figure out she wasn't da wife. Poor woman died a few years back."

"It was a pleasant surprise," Ben said, remembering back to the first day he'd seen her with her hood down. Is that when he'd fallen? Had it happened so quickly?

* * *

KITTY WORKED on a pair of gloves for the shop while Ben read Byron aloud. He stopped reciting and closed the book.

"You don't enjoy Byron, do you?" he asked.

Kitty shrugged, giving him a side-glance. "He's fine.

I'm just not much for poetry. I enjoy listening to you, though." She wore a pale-yellow muslin that complemented her eyes and dark hair by contrast. "Don't stop."

He sighed, then checked his pocket watch again just as a knock sounded on the back door. He rose to answer it but realized it wasn't his house. Genie and Lydia had gone with Mr. Lockwood to a concert. Ben hadn't seen anyone as smitten as the stablemaster. The man doted on Lydia Peckton.

"If you don't mind, may I answer that? I've arranged for a surprise for you."

Kitty's head jerked up. "A surprise? For me?" She set her work on the table and stared at him. "Is it a delivery?"

"Of a type. You'll see," Ben said, excited to see her reaction. He dashed down the stairs and opened the door.

"Took you long enough," said Nora, pushing past him and heading up the stairs with the great gray beast at her side. Her long red hair was pulled back with a ribbon and shone copper against the black of her pelisse.

"Wait for me. I want to see her expression!" Ben hurried after his sister. "And you haven't been introduced properly."

Nora grinned at him over her shoulder. "Do you really think that's necessary?"

Then Kitty was at the top of the stairs, gasping and clapping. "This must be Aonarach!" She held the door wide for the guests to enter.

"And you must be Miss Felton," said Nora, her green eyes studying Kitty. "I'm the famous sister."

"The actress who will be on the same stage as Charles Macready!" Kitty took her hand and shook it. "I'm honored to meet you, Miss O'Brien."

Nora waggled her brows at her brother as they followed Kitty into the parlor. "Let's not be stiff. I'm Honora, Nora to my friends. If Ben is officially courting you, we'll soon be closer than the latest passengers on a stagecoach."

"I'm Katherine Felton, Kitty to my friends. Please make yourself comfortable." Kitty turned her attention to Aonarach. With two hands, she scrubbed the animal's ruff. His wet tongue ran up her face in gratitude. She wrinkled her nose at the smell, wiped her cheek with a sleeve, and chuckled. "I'm afraid if I sit down, you'll be taller than me."

"Da has taught him to mind his manners. He'll sit, so it won't be so awkward. Meant to warn you his breath is atrocious. Gus gave him a sardine before we left." Nora shuddered. "I hate those salty fish."

"Would you like some tea? Wine? I believe we have some sherry in the kitchen," offered Kitty.

"Sherry would be lovely, thanks," said Nora, laughing when the wolfhound followed Kitty.

"I love you, Sister," Ben said, the ridiculous grin forming again. "I knew Kitty would enjoy this."

"I'm to bring back every detail of this visit with a meticulous description of Miss Felton. *She's lovely,"* whispered Nora.

"Let me go help her with the drinks," he said,

pleased that Nora approved. “She may have difficulty maneuvering around the beast.”

When he entered the kitchen, Kitty turned with hands on her hips. “You thoughtful, wonderful, dear man.” Then she handed him the tray. “We’ll be right in.”

Ben stood, the compliment still penetrating his brain as Kitty held up a biscuit and tried to get Aonarach to lay.

“Lie down,” she commanded, the treat in hand as she added a motion to the order. The dog’s head moved with the biscuit.

Ben shook his head. “He was taught commands in Gaelic. Sit is *suigh*.” The dog sat, now looking up at Ben. “You try it.”

“Sig?” she said as a question, holding the biscuit up again.

The wolfhound thumped his tail, his head moving back and forth between the humans asking him to perform a task he was already doing.

Kitty broke off a piece and held it on her palm. The dog gingerly took it from her hand. “He’s so gentle.”

“He’s an ancient breed, used for hunting and guarding. The motto is ‘gentle when stroked, fierce when provoked.’ Aonarach is a good representation of the breed.”

“I have half a biscuit left. What else shall I have him do?” she asked.

“Tell him to lie down again but in Gaelic. I’ll say it in parts, so he doesn’t put them together. Lee… she… uss.”

“Luigh síos!” Kitty cooed to the dog when he

obeyed and gave him the rest of the treat. "You could eat my Terry for a snack!"

Once they were settled in the parlor, Kitty once again giving Aonarach the command to lie down, Ben sipped the sherry and listened as his sister and Kitty chatted. Nora had warmed to Kitty with the first compliment, sensing it was sincere. She told several amusing stories about various productions she'd been a part of.

"I tried to talk Da into letting me bring the beast for a performance, but he refused. I was in a comedy and wanted to dress him up, have him howl along with the chorus." Nora grinned. "Did you know the dog can sing?"

Kitty shook her head, anticipation shining in her violet eyes. "I have a penny whistle if you'd need accompaniment."

"Yes!"

Kitty hurried to her room and took her seat again. "What are we playing?"

"'Comin' Through the Rye.' Do you know it?"

"Of course." She put the whistle to her lips and blew the first notes as Nora began to sing.

*If a body meet a body,*
*Comin' thro the rye,*
*If a body kiss a body,*
*Need a body cryyyyyy?*

Aonarach raised his head and gave a mournful howl along with "cry." Nora's clear voice continued,

*Ev'ry lassie has her laddie,*
*Nane, they say, ha'e I,*

*Yet a' the lads they smile on me,*

*When comin' thro' the ryyyyye.*

This time Ben added his wail to the dog's, pleased that Kitty could barely suppress her laughter and keep up the tune.

"So, what's your opinion? Should he have a debut on the stage?" asked Nora.

"Aonarach, yes. Ben, absolutely not," said Kitty, breaking into a gale of laughter.

*Yes,* he thought, *this is just what she needed.* A feeling of contentment spread over him as he watched his sister patter with the woman he lov—

His mouth went dry. *Blast and perdition!* Did he love her? He'd only known her a month. He was attracted to her, considered her a good match, enjoyed her company... but love so soon?

*Your feet will bring you to where your heart is.*

Where had his feet taken him every night this week?

Demmed Irish sayings!

# CHAPTER 13

*Two days later*
*The Dog's Bone*

"Hope he got the worst of it," said Ben, studying Roger's colorful and swollen eye. "Are you all right?"

"Fine. Ma kept it from puffin' up too bad." Lynch took a drink of his ale. "Good news and bad news. What do you want first?"

"Bad news," said Ben and Clayton together.

"The second traitor is dead."

Clayton cursed. "And?"

"The toady who Rowlands sent to follow the traitor is now being held at the Brown Bear. The honorable Mr. Ruthven will personally be watching over him once Harry is done with the interrogation." Roger grinned, winced, then gingerly patted his aggrieved eye. "And this canary will sing."

The Brown Bear was a tavern on Bow Street across from the main constabulary. The cellar of the public house contained cells for the temporary holding of criminals. George Ruthven, a third-generation—and the present—constable for the district, had his own table at the establishment.

Clayton sat back in his chair, staring at Roger. "Devilish good job. So tell us!"

Roger explained how he followed the "canary" to The Grapes near the Limehouse docks. When the bloke came out of the tavern, he was tailing another man. Then who appears behind them? Rowlands.

"Both the scallywags moved up quickly behind the traitor, grabbed an arm on each side, and forced him into an alley. I caught up just in time to see Rowlands point a gun at a man's head and pull the trigger." Roger moved his hands excitedly as he spoke. "Rowlands's toady spotted me, holding me at bay while his boss escaped."

"That how you got the black eye?" asked Ben.

Roger nodded. "The lickspittle popped out of the shadow and got the first blow. Just enough time for Rowlands to run. I got the second punch, and it was over."

Roger was known for his fighting skills, especially his right hook.

"You're sure it was Rowlands?" asked Clayton.

"Without a doubt. His scar is very helpful," said Roger, drawing a finger down the side of his face.

"You'd think he'd be more careful. He's as identifiable as Gus with his gigantism."

Gus wasn't afflicted with any disease. He was naturally large like Paddy, but Ben had to laugh. He would be putting a case together for Marshall. Not that the man being held could lead them to The Vicar, but the more knowledge they had, the closer they got. It was like a long chess game, putting each piece in the correct place.

"I'm curious to see what Rowlands has to say when we meet tonight. I've managed to stay with the counterfeiting duty rather than roughing up customers who aren't paying their share for protection." Clayton finished his ale and slammed down the bumper. "I'm happy not to be a party to that, but I'm also not seeing as much when I'm tucked away producing fake coins."

Ben could hear the agitation in his best friend's voice but was relieved Clayton wouldn't have to witness innocents being hurt. The Peelers had decided against shutting down any more individual counterfeit operations since the outfits opened somewhere else within a few weeks. Rather than waste time finding the new location, Paddy hoped the remaining few would lead them to The Vicar.

"Do you think the Feltons are safe now?" he asked Clayton.

"Let's see what Harry finds out. If Rowlands is trying to locate any witnesses—Lynch, here, excluded—we'll know soon enough."

"If they are still in danger, do you think The Vicar knows of Kitty?" This was his worst fear.

Clayton shook his head. "Rowlands wouldn't want him to know of loose ends until they're all tied in a tidy knot."

* * *

*NEXT DAY*
*Chancery Lane*

BEN WALKED from his office to Holborn, searching the heavy traffic for a hackney. He gave the direction to Millard's East India House at 16 Cheapside. Genie had told him it was the ideal place to purchase a few special supplies for Kitty. Items she would use for herself or someone special.

He knew Kitty's favorite color was green, and with her personality, he assumed she would prefer a vibrant shade. Genie and Lydia had given him some advice as to what he might purchase, and he reached for his notebook where he'd written down the items. When the hackney pulled to a stop in front of the East India House, Ben gawked up at the huge building. All that space for cloth?

He entered a huge hall filled with dozens of customers. Giant bolts of cloth, stored in hollow spaces near the ceiling, lined the two walls above the long counters where smartly dressed, all-male clerks assisted the clientele. Long lengths were pulled from the bolts to drape across the walls so they could be pulled to an interested customer for inspection. There were muslins, satins, silks, tweeds, and linens of all colors imaginable, and various prints sported the flora and fauna of England and countries abroad. The noise level was high as people bickered about price or chatted with one another while they waited their turn.

*I'm quite out of my element,* thought Ben, joining a queue in front of a wall of shelves filled with bins of accessories. Conversations floated within hearing.

"Not that one, the blue above it."

"You can't really expect me to pay that much!"

"Will there be anything else, ma'am?"

Ben soon found himself enthralled with the hectic atmosphere. Huge swaths of brightly patterned cloth would be pulled from the wall, across a counter, and in front of the customer for inspection. Then the same would be rolled up again, and another would be unfurled.

"How may I assist you, sir?" asked the mustached, red-haired clerk.

Ben slapped down the list and gave the man a sheepish smile. "I need a variety of these for a gift."

*silk or satin ribbons*

*silk flowers, roses, small posies*

*feathers*

*delicate lace and netting*

*beads*

*paste gems*

*clusters of berries or fruit*

*gimp braid*

He explained the purpose of the gift and what Kitty created with the items.

"Very good, sir. Give me an idea of what you'd like to spend, and I'll choose an assortment of items for you."

"Would a sovereign be enough?" he asked, not wanting to spend too much and make Kitty anxious.

"Yes, sir." The man turned his back and began selecting items and placing them on a tray. He climbed a ladder that moved back and forth, like the type used in a bookshop, and soon had a nice collection.

"Would you like any cloth to go with these?" asked the clerk.

"How much and what type of cloth would make a green reticule?" He wanted Kitty to make something for herself, knowing it would be better than anything he could possibly buy.

With his purchases wrapped and tucked under his arm, Ben left the warehouse and joined the throng of people still filling the main thoroughfare. He wanted to stop in and visit with Mr. Felton, but Clayton had advised him not to be seen there. Ben might end up being followed.

Now that the mornings didn't include Kitty's bright smile, he'd decided he didn't need a knocker-up. He felt silly having the older man wake him up. So unless Ben found Felton in the evening while on his route, he didn't see him.

Once home, he settled into the parlor with a glass of brandy and a book. He'd rather be with Kitty, but the three women had an emergency order, and they were working extra hours today. When his lids drooped, he decided to go to his room and find sleep early.

As he unwrapped his cravat, idly wondering about men who didn't dress themselves, he saw Mr. Felton passing by in his usual garb: long coat, lantern, and a thick staff for protection. Terry was at his heels, then in front, then next to him. As the duo progressed up the lane, he watched as the dog trotted to an opening between two buildings, staring at something. But when Felton called in a harsh voice, Terry obeyed and followed his master, the hackles on his neck raised. They disappeared into the night, the lantern a faint yellow glow.

Wondering what the canine had seen, Ben lingered at the window. He was rewarded with a figure in dark clothing coming out of the alley, moving in the same direction. The devil! He was following Felton. Ben was sure of it. He tossed his cravat on the bed, went to his wardrobe, and retrieved his pistol, tucking it into his waistband before donning his coat.

Ben hurried down the stairs and onto the street, heading in the same direction as the trio he'd observed. It had been several years since he'd done any surveillance, and he had to slow his step once he caught sight of the lone figure. He couldn't see Felton or the dog.

The man turned to the right. Ben heard the sound of glass breaking and hurried his pace. When he came to the street, it was dark. He heard the low growl before he saw the dark forms ahead. Ben kept to the other side of the street, staying in the shadows. Felton was pushed against the wall of a brick building, holding his hand out to quiet Terry.

*He doesn't want the man to hurt the dog,* Ben thought, knowing Felton worried about Kitty. He wasn't sure if the assailant had a pistol or a blade, so he worked his way slowly. If he surprised the man too early, he might panic. A blade might slip or a gun might go off. When he was directly across from them, Terry hyperfocused on his master's next command, Ben slipped up behind them.

Felton saw him and began talking to his attacker. "I don't know what you're talking about. I don't have a daughter."

"You have the dog, so you know where the girl is," rasped the man. He lifted a hand and pointed the muzzle of a gun at Felton's head.

To his credit, the older man remained calm. "You must have me confused with someone else."

"Then I'll kill the first witness," said the man, turning the gun toward the dog.

Felton took the opportunity and threw his weight against the man. He fell backward into Ben, who wrapped his arm around the man's neck. Terry sank his teeth into the man's leg. "I wouldn't move if I were you," said Ben. "I'm a bit giddy with the trigger."

"I have manacles," said Felton, patting his long coat and producing the iron wristlets. As he reached for the criminal's hand, the man threw his head back and cracked Ben's forehead, then crouched and ran head-first into the night watchman.

"Bloody Charley," the assailant yelled as Felton toppled to the ground, running toward the next street.

Terry ran to Felton, and Ben went after the

assailant. It wasn't necessary. Gus appeared at the corner, his big form blocking the exit. With an arm held out, his meaty fist snared the man's neck and lifted him off the ground.

"Where you off to in such a hurry? My friends ain't finished speaking with you yet." Gus seized the back of the man's collar, then put him in a bear hold, rendering the ruffian harmless.

"You'll be sorry," yelled the man, trying to kick at Gus. "You don't know who I work for."

Ben could now see the zigzag scar down the man's cheek. A weight lifted from his shoulders as his brain took in the fact that they had caught the murderer. He stumbled, righted himself, then backtracked to help Felton up.

"I'm fine, son," said the night watchman. "Let's get that bugger secured."

It was another hour before Rowlands was safely locked away in the bowels of the Brown Bear. Harry Walters was summoned, and he and George Ruthven, the main constable for Bow Street, decided to keep Gus watching over the cells. Harry didn't want to take a chance on another man dying in custody.

"It's good to see you again, Sir Harry," Ruthven said, holding out his hand. They had worked together a few years back, uncovering the Cato Conspiracy. Even at this late hour, the man wore his signature yellow waistcoat. "How's O'Brien?"

"Well, sir," said Harry. "You should stop in and have a drink with him sometime."

"I might just do that," he said. "Now I think I'll return home and rewarm my bed."

Once Ruthven left, Harry turned to Ben and Mr. Felton. "Gus and I will finish questioning the prisoner. I'll contact you if we learn anymore. Go home, both of you, and get some rest."

"Is it safe to bring my daughter home now?" asked Felton.

Harry nodded. "First thing in the morning."

Ben and Felton walked out of the public house. Terry was waiting at the door for them, his tail spinning frantically when he saw them. The pup ran and jumped against his owner's thighs, then leaped again. The night watchman caught him and held him close.

"Good boy," he said into the dog's scruffy fur.

"He is, indeed," agreed Ben. "It was pure luck that I saw you pass by my house. Terry was focused on something in the alley, so I watched for a while. Someone emerged and followed you. I grabbed my pistol and decided to make sure you were fine."

"Not sure what would have happened if you hadn't." Felton set the dog down and gave Ben a side hug. "You saved my life, son. I don't think he had any intention of letting me live."

"I'm just relieved Kitty will soon be home. Nothing could make her happier."

"I don't know about that," said Mr. Felton, squeezing Ben's shoulder.

Ben took a hackney back to his room. As he replayed the events in his mind, he remembered his words to Mr. Felton.

*It was pure luck I saw you pass by my house.*
*Pure luck.*

# CHAPTER 14

*Madame Chapelle's*
*Clements Lane*

Kitty blinked and rubbed her eyes, stretching her arms over her head. She could hear voices, probably in the kitchen. Had she overslept? A male voice rose above the others.

*Pa.*

She tossed back the counterpane and pulled on her robe. By the time her fingers touched the handle, something was scratching the other side of the door. When she opened it, Terry's wagging tail and wiggling body greeted her with an excited bark. She fell to her knees and hugged him, tears spilling down her cheeks.

Holding him in her arms, Kitty ran down the short hall and burst into the kitchen. Her father was there, cap in his hand, still wearing his long coat from his last shift. She set Terry down and threw herself into her father's arms, her breaths coming in short gasps.

"I missed you so, so much," she cried into his neck. "Is it over? Tell me it's over." She hugged him with all her might as he twirled her in a circle.

"Time for you to come home, luv," he said.

Her heart pounded, happiness welling up in her chest and spilling over in more tears. When he finally loosened his hold, and her feet were firmly back on the floor, she turned to her new friends.

Like her, Genie and Lydia both wore their night-clothes and mobcaps.

"We will miss you," said Lydia, holding out her arms.

"But we'll see you almost every day," added Genie, waiting for her turn to hug Kitty.

"Pa—" She turned around to face her father again as Ben entered from the parlor.

"There's the hero of the day," said her father.

"Hero?" she asked, staring at the handsome man who had stolen her heart. Kitty longed to fling herself into his arms, but there were *so* many people in the small space.

"His quick thinking saved my life. Didn't know he even owned a pistol," Pa told everyone.

"A p-pistol?" Fear caught in her throat. How close had she come to losing the men she loved? Because she'd admitted to herself this week that she was madly, crazy in love with Mr. Benjamin Cooper.

"Never used it," Ben said, taking a step closer.

His brown-gold eyes studied her, then he held out

his arms. "I don't care if this is appropriate or not," he said, his voice husky.

"I believe I'll serve tea in the parlor. Mr. Felton, would you join us?" asked Lydia.

Her father grinned. "Delighted to."

Kitty almost knocked the poor man over when the room was empty. "I knew you would fix everything. I knew I could trust you." She kissed him on his mouth, his cheeks, his chin, his nose. "Thank you!"

Ben loosened his hold and let her slide back down to the floor. His gaze locked with hers, as if proving to himself she was there, then bent his head to kiss her. He pressed his lips to hers, and she kissed him back.

"I brought you a present," he murmured against her hair.

"I'm starting to enjoy surprises," she said, putting her hands behind back. "Should I close my eyes?"

"Yes."

She did but heard him walk away, then return.

"Open your eyes," he said.

She did, and he was holding a large package wrapped in brown paper. Kitty raised a questioning brow but took the package and sat at the table. Ben joined her as she untied the string.

"Oh my," she gasped as she peeked in small pouches holding wonderful goodies. There were beads and feathers and tiny braiding... a treasure trove of supplies that would have cost a small fortune.

Two swaths of cloth, one of satin in rifle green and one of silk in Pomona green, were the perfect amount to make two reticules.

"Your favorite color is green, but I wasn't sure what shade. So the man at the East India Company said he would choose a dark and a bright."

Kitty blinked back tears. "You went to Millard's to buy all this for me? It's too much."

"No, it's not. And don't cry," he said, panic in his tawny eyes. "I wanted to make you smile."

"Happy tears, you ninny," she murmured. "You don't mind courting a woman who has aspirations other than being a wife?" The answer to this question could change her life.

"You met Nora. She was raised by Maggie. Can you imagine any male telling them they couldn't pursue their dream?" He reached over and tipped her chin up. "I want you to be happy, Kitty." He leaned forward and kissed her softly as her arms curled around his neck.

"My good luck charm," she whispered in his ear.

"And you may be mine," he told her, kissing her again.

* * *

*May 1821*

*St. Clement's Church*

"I NOW PRONOUNCE you man and wife," the vicar announced to the congregation.

Clayton kissed Genie, and Kitty quit trying to stem the tears. She let them fall freely for her friend.

Lydia squeezed her hand. "I've been through two handkerchiefs already. Lud, how I love that girl."

Kitty hugged her, then turned to wait for Ben, who had stood up for Clayton. He stopped in the aisle to escort her out into the bright morning. He was dressed to the nines in black tails, violet waistcoat (to match her eyes), and a pristine white cravat. Behind them, Lydia followed on George Lockwood's arm.

Genie confided that the man's eyes had misted when her aunt requested that he escort her to the ceremony. Perhaps another wedding was on the way?

"Congratulations!" The cries echoed in St. Clement's Church as the newly wedded couple departed the building. The people who loved them most called out their well-wishes.

Lydia began to cry again, George patting her hand. Maggie and Nora were wiping away tears too. Paddy and Gus were grinning. Harry and Sampson were both there, lopsided smiles on their faces, an arm protectively around their wives.

They had labored for weeks on a wedding dress of the palest rose; the intricate ivory lace overlay so delicate Kitty had been afraid to touch it at first. The lace had come from Italy, a gift from Genie's father and stepmother, Lord and Lady Winston.

Clayton was so handsome in his slate coattails, his auburn curls barely tamed, and his moss-green eyes shining with love.

The couple laughed at the worn shoe thrown by Eli. A sign of good luck that Mr. and Mrs. Pierce hopefully wouldn't need. They would honeymoon in Paris, another wedding present from Genie's father.

Clayton dodged another old shoe thrown by Roger.

"May ye have a dram of the happiness I've had with my Maggie," Paddy said, hugging them both, then kissing his wife on the mouth with a loud smack.

As they left for the wedding breakfast, held in the O'Brien's backyard with tents to protect them from the sun, Kitty gazed across the street at Madame Chapelle's. She would help Lydia run the shop while Genie and Clayton were on the Continent.

The carriage lurched forward, and Ben moved next to her on the squab. "I've never seen him so happy."

"I thought Nora and Gus were riding with us." She peered out the window. "What happened?" Her father was meeting them at the O'Briens.

When she turned around, Ben was holding a small box. His silly, lopsided smile was identical to his brother's, a smile formed of love. Kitty smiled, her hand moving to her chest as if to protect her heart.

"Miss Katherine Felton, the loveliest, cleverest of women. I always thought I was luckless. A man who providence passed by, who never had a chance playing the odds." He swallowed. "But I've found my lucky charm, and I hope to keep her by my side for the rest of my days."

Her hand went to her mouth, joy bubbling up her throat and spilling out as tears. She began nodding her head as he opened the box.

"Will you marry me? Will you be my wife, the mother of my children, and the maker of my clothes?"

She began to laugh, wiping her cheeks. “Yes, you ridiculous man. Yes, I will marry you.”

# CHAPTER 15

## THE VICAR

*June 1821*
*London*

He was glad to be back in Town. It had been a shame to lose two more of his fold to the gallows. But there were always men who needed blunt and would do almost anything to get it.

"Come in," he called at the knock.

DB entered with another man, immediately making him wary.

"You didn't mention bringing a guest," he said, his tone neutral.

"I thought I'd surprise you," said DB.

The "surprise" moved forward, pulling off his cap to show his snow-white hair, ice-blue eyes, and a wicked smile.

"Johns," said The Vicar, standing and holding out his hand. "Where the devil did he find you?"

"Got a note saying the major was short on men." He gave The Vicar a salute. "Volunteering for duty, Lord Major."

"I accept," he said, a smile curling his lips. "I'm in desperate need of someone to lead my congregation."

"DB said you've exchanged ranks," said Johns.

After a short discussion—these men didn't need their hands held—he left for the theater. Once settled in his box, he waited for the curtain to open, thinking about his DB and Johns.

They had served with him in the war. Men of courage and strength who couldn't comprehend the word "no." DB, a brilliant marksman, was born to be an assassin. Quiet, unassuming, able to slip in and out of a crowded place and never be noticed.

Johns's personality was the opposite. Jovial and charming, he was able to gather men around him and demand allegiance. But disobey an order or threaten the safety of his commander, and those clear-blue eyes could turn deadly in a breath. Their loyalty was unquestioned. All three had saved each other's lives more than once. None of them would have survived Waterloo without the trio staying together.

Yes, the tide was changing. He realized the curtain had risen and focused on the stage. When a supporting actress took the stage, he blinked.

*Who was that divine creature?*

Glorious hair the color of an expensive burgundy. Green eyes richer than emeralds.

Then she spoke, and her sensuous voice enveloped him. He drew in a deep breath, his pulse racing as if he'd run the entire length of Rotten Row. No woman had affected him like this.

He peered over his shoulder and beckoned his man with the crook of a finger. "Find out what her name is and if she's married." Not that it mattered.

He listened to her as she sang, her voice like an angel. He was enchanted by this vivacious woman. His eyes scanned the crowd and noticed other men watching her, wanting her. Jealousy burned in his gut.

"Her name is Miss Honora O'Brien," his man said upon returning. "She is not married and will also be performing later this month."

The Vicar smiled and settled back in his chair to enjoy the play. He may become a more frequent visitor of the theater.

As she left the stage, he decided he would have her. Miss Honora O'Brien would be his.

# AUTHOR'S NOTE

As a reader, I always enjoy knowing what parts of the story are factual history. In this story:

**Knocker-up/Knocker-uppers**

This line of work did not truly become popular for another decade. The Industrial Revolution drew more and more people into the cities, and factory workers had strict time schedules. Alarm clocks had not yet been invented. So British and Irish entrepreneurs (usually women or elderly men) came up with a profitable solution.

For a few pence a week, a person would wake each morning with the assistance of a knocker-up. Tools of the trade included pea shooters to shoot dried peas at the window or long thin willow sticks to tap it. Both devices made noise without breaking the pane.

Knocker-ups became vital, as missing a shift meant a loss of wages. Losing one day's pay could be the difference between paying rent or being on the street.

**Chimney sweeps and boy climbers:**

Young boys were used to climb up the flues of chimneys to sweep them clean of soot. Children as young as four were often used because of their size and flexibility. At one time, London employed between 500-600 climbing boys.

It was a dangerous job. Climbers could become stuck in the maze of connecting flues. (Chimneys, not flues, were taxed, so additional flues were often installed to avoid the additional annual cost.) Tales of brick walls being disassembled to retrieve the bodies of young boys was not uncommon. They could be burned, bones broken, bruised or killed while working in the dangerous, narrow brick chimneys. Non-fatal maladies included reduced vision, swollen joints, stooped backs, and "sweep's cancer" or "soot wart"—a carcinoma of the skin of the scrotum.

Historian James Kelly writes that "society at large chose to overlook the abuses that were an inevitable consequence" of the necessity of chimney-sweeping. Most people were "largely accepting of the child injuries and, on occasion, child fatalities that were a feature of the trade." So when James Murphy of Dublin beat his nine-year-old apprentice, Patrick Usher, to death in 1777, he didn't expect to be prosecuted, let alone executed for the murder.

The abuse was so horrific, the authorities deemed it necessary to intervene. As the late eighteenth century dawned into the early nineteenth century, what had previously been acceptable became unacceptable.

The Chimney Sweepers Act of 1788 raised the

minimum age of a climber to eight. Though it was little enforced, public opinion was changing. As society's toleration of abuse diminished, more humanitarian groups formed to defend children and the poor who had been ignored and disregarded. There was a string of reform bills throughout the nineteenth century, but the practice was not officially abolished until the Chimney Sweepers Acts (Repeal) Act of 1938.

**William Charles Macready**

Mr. Macready was a well-established leading tragedy actor during the Regency period. He performed twice in June of 1821 at the Theatre Royal in Covent-Garden. On June 8, Macready held a Benefit Night, a traditional performance where all proceeds went directly to the actor, usually in his most famous roles. On June 10, Macready recreated his notable portrayal of Shakespear's *Henry V*, and Thomas Morton's *The Slave* was presented on June 20. I thought it was fun to include Nora in the cast.

**George Ruthven and the Brown Bear**

George Ruthven was the principal Bow Street officer (and constable) during this story. He was also the leader of the 21 February raid that ended the Cato Street Conspiracy. (Harry Walters received his knighthood for his participation in Crimes, Conspiracies, and Courtship. He was known for always wearing a bright canary waistcoat.

The Brown Bear was a pub across the road from the Bow Street Office. Since there were no formal jails within the districts, the pub was often used for the temporary holding of criminals during interrogation or while waiting to be brought before the magistrate. It doubled as a hub of informers for the Runners. Drink was a tool often used for intelligence gathering and the alehouse was vital to the Runners for this purpose. Runners and constables often waited at the Brown Bear when on call.

# ABOUT THE AUTHOR

USA Today Bestselling author Aubrey Wynne resides in the Midwest with her husband, dogs, horses, mule, and barn cats. Obsessions include wine, history, travel, trail riding, and all things Christmas. Her Chicago Christmas series and historical romances have received multiple awards and nominations as a Rone finalist by InD'tale Magazine.

Aubrey's first love is medieval romance but after dipping her toe in the Regency period in 2018 with the *Wicked Earls' Club,* she was smitten. This inspired her sweet Regency spin-off series *Once Upon a Widow,* and a steamy Scottish Regency series, *A MacNaughton Castle Romance.* Her Regency detective series, *Paddy's Peelers,* will launched in 2025.

Social Media Links:

Website:
http://www.aubreywynne.com
Facebook:
https://www.facebook.com/magnificentvalor
Aubrey's Ever After Facebook group:

https://www.facebook.com/groups/AubreyWynnesEverAfters/

Twitter:

https://twitter.com/Aubreywynne51

Pinterest:

https://www.pinterest.com/aubreywynne51/

Instagram:

https://www.instagram.com/Aubreywynne51

Bookbub page:

https://www.bookbub.com/profile/aubrey-wynne

Goodreads:

https://www.goodreads.com/author/show/7383937.Aubrey_Wynne

Sign up for my newsletter and don't miss future releases

https://www.subscribepage.com/k3f1z5

## ALSO BY AUBREY WYNNE

**Once Upon a Widow series**

**Earl of Sunderland #1**

**Maggie award, International Digital Awards finalist**

Christopher Roker inherited the title of rake. She hides behind her independence. Fate accepts the challenge…

Escaping his late brother's memory, Lady Grace is a welcome distraction. But as the attraction grows, Kit finds himself wavering between his old military life and the lure of an exceptional but unwilling woman.

**A Wicked Earl's Widow #2**

**Recommended by InD'tale Magazine**

Eliza, Lady Sunderland, is widowed after one year. Her abusive father, near financial ruin, is already planning another wedding.

When Viscount Pendleton discovers a beauty defending an elderly woman against ruffians, he is smitten. But Nate soon realizes he must discover Eliza's dark past to save the woman he loves.

**Rhapsody and Rebellion #3**

**Maggie finalist, nominated for Rone Award, InD'tale Magazine**

A Scottish legacy... A political rebellion... Two hearts destined to meet...

Alisabeth was betrothed from the cradle. At seventeen, she marries her best friend and finds happiness if not passion. In less than a year, a political rebellion makes her a widow. The handsome English earl arrives a month later and rouses her desire and a terrible guilt.

Crossing the border into Scotland, Gideon finds his predictable world turned upside down. Folklore, legend, and political unrest intertwine with an unexpected attraction to a feisty Highland beauty. When the earl learns of an English plot to stir the Scots into rebellion, he must choose his country or save the clan and the woman who stirs his soul.

**Earl of Darby #4**

**Holt Medallion Winner, NTRWA Reader's Choice Award, Nominated for Rone Award, InD'tale magazine**

Miss Hannah Pendleton, nursing her pride after her childhood crush falls in love with another, hurls herself into the excitement of a first season.

Since his wife's suicide on their wedding night, the Earl of Darby has carefully cultivated his rakish reputation. But when Nicholas sees a lovely newcomer being courted by the devil himself, her innocence and candor revive the chivalry buried deep in his soul.

**Earl of Brecken #5**

He's on the brink of ruin. She's in search of a hero.

Notorious for his seductive charm, the Earl of Brecken searches for a wealthy heiress. His choices are dismal until he meets Miss Franklin. Guileless, gorgeous and with an enormous dowry, she seems the answer to his prayers. Until his conscience makes an unexpected appearance.

**Earl of Griffith #6**

*Sorrow and Regrets...*

After eloping, a widowed Lady Helen is disillusioned with love and raising a three-year-old alone. Now she must face the music and her family.

*An unexpected ray of sunshine...*

Conway, Earl of Griffith is smitten at first sight with his friend's sister and adorable daughter. But can he convince the grieving and lovely widow that love is worth a second chance?

**Beware A Wallflower's Wrath #7**

Annis Craigg gave her heart—and innocence—away at seventeen. When Lord Robert Harding returns to Scotland fifteen years later, he's desperate to find the only woman he's ever loved. But she has secrets and an attitude.

Lies, secrets, and betrayal will challenge the fierce love of a steadfast Highlander and remorseful but determined Englishman. Will destiny find a way to bring two star-crossed souls together?

**A Wallflower's Wassail Punch #8**

Lady Annette's first Season was a disaster after a duke's son pinched her by the punchbowl, and she walloped him in the nose. Five years of malicious rumors later, her father offers an outrageous dowry so he too can marry.

Lord Wilkinson, a widower, meets a striking, intelligent woman, with a dry wit only he seems to appreciate. His heart stirs for the first time in decades. But will their age difference and wagging tongues interfere with their budding romance?

**The Scoundrel's Christmas Challenge #9**

*A contest to win her fortune...*

Lady Winfield, a long-time wealthy widow, is infamous for her outrageous house parties. While hosting her annual Christmastide gathering, Christiana proposes a new game: a daily challenge of her choice. She will accept the proposal of the man who can best her at three or more competitions by Twelfth Night. Though all agree to the diversion, no one expects the games to include marksmanship, archery, and fencing.

*A contest to win her heart...*

When Lucius, Viscount Bolingbroke presents Lady Winfield with a secret challenge, she can't resist. Will their midnight rendezvous and private contests end in certain victory for one or a dual attraction for both?

**The Duplicate Duke #10**

*In a country far, far away...*

Lady Gwendolyn Beaumaris and her brother have been known as the Downing twins since their father's death when they were eight years old. At twenty-two, Gwen and her mother have settled in Boston while her brother tries to make his fortune in the fur trade. Down to their last pennies, she must consider marriage to a wealthy middle-aged merchant.

*The brass ring is so close...*

Lord Wickton has worked tirelessly the past two years to bring honor back to the family name. When the viscount learns he is the heir presumptive to his great uncle's dukedom, his prayers are answered.

*A comedy of errors...*

When a letter arrives announcing that Gwen's brother is the new Duke of Shackerley, mother and daughter come up with a desperate plan: Gwendolyn will impersonate her brother and assume the dukedom. But when the sinfully handsome Wickton meets them at the dock, and Gwen is hopelessly smitten.

*A tale of love, deception, and the power of fate will entangle a desperate viscount with a daring female. Can he forgive her charade, or will he snuff out the burning passion that rages in her heart.*

**Merry Mazes and Mistletoe Magic #11**

*A debutante's rude awakening...*

Lady Jennet Gordon has led a charmed life until her first Season. Rumors about her father's finances circulate, followed by a tragic but suspicious accident, leaving Jenny and her mother a modest widow's dowery to survive on with no immediate heir. Two years later, secluded on their Northumberland estate, a distant cousin is found to assume the title. Jenny fears that the heir—known in the shipping industry as the Hangman—will evict her and her mother from their home. Surely, he would not throw them out at Christmastide?

*A driven man with a fierce reputation...*

Barnabus Gordon is the grandson of a pirate and the son of a privateer. His grandfather, the younger son of a titled family, refused to accept the traditional careers offered him and took to the sea. When Barnabus's father is killed early in the war, he vows to legitimize the family business. Using the cutthroat lessons learned in his childhood from two generations of rebellious Gordons, he buys out shipowners in financial distress and accrues his own fleet. When Barnabus learns he is the new Earl of Townsen, a title that is debt-ridden and comes with two penniless females.

*A collision beneath the mistletoe...*

The gruffly handsome Gordon is determined to settle the issue of his newly acquired English estate and return to the sea. Yet when he arrives at Brierdene Hall, he discovers two caring women and a forgotten longing for love and family. With both of them hiding their growing affection—and past secrets—Lady Jennet worries her feelings for Barnabus will appear too convenient. He fears moving forward because of their familial ties. Until the Town lady and seafaring brute find themselves sixes and sevens under a mistletoe. One kiss ignites a Yule log of passion and holiday magic that refuses to be extinguished.

**Kiss the Scoundrel Farewell #12**

Lady Margaret marries out of duty only to find herself in the center of a scandal. Her husband, Baron Drake, dies in a duel over another woman. With no children and no desire to be shackled again, Meg decides to enjoy life as men do. She will be the other woman instead of the wife held captive by the whims of a man. Lady Drake enjoys the freedom of her widow's status.

Simon, Lord Hayward, a dutiful son with no fantasies of love, agrees to marry a wealthy heiress to plump the family's coffers. His father, in love with his mistress for decades, sets out to find his son one of his own. Simon scoffs at the idea, but when he meets an alluring courtesan at a masquerade, he finds himself smitten.

In a twist of fate, the masks come off, and Simon and Meg realize they met years ago, sharing a kiss in a duke's garden. Their secrets come out: She is no courtesan, and he is betrothed. After the viscount confesses his love, the baroness flees for the safety of the countryside.

As Lady Drake begins to doubt her scheme of being a

paramour, Lord Hayward wonders if he can be happy with a wife who is not Meg and searches her out. He seeks her out only to find danger lurking in the idyllic English hills, and they soon learn the past has consequences no matter who you pretend to be.

**A Paddy's Peelers Mystery series**

*Set in the hectic district of Cheapside during the Regency, Paddy's Peelers search the dregs of London with skill and cunning to bring criminals to justice and, perhaps, unexpectedly find love along the way. A sweet but action-packed romance.*

**Crime, Conspiracies, and Courtship #1**

Lady Matilda has always been an introvert, preferring her books to awkward conversations with strangers. As her first Season arrives, her mother insists she put away her bluestocking and concentrate on finding a husband. But Mattie is terrified of finding herself betrothed or even worse — not betrothed. The arrogant men of the ton terrify her.

Mr. Harry Walters is an orphaned, ex-Bow Street runner turned investigator, who makes a living by his wits. Working for Paddy O'Brien and his Peelers, often taking assignments for the Home Office, Walters is used to working closely with the beau monde. When a peer approaches him about a new assignment, Harry realizes they are both after the same man. He accepts the job but soon finds himself also protecting the earl's sister.

While working in costume at a masquerade, Walters makes a fatal mistake when he asks Lady Matilda to dance. It takes only a few stolen glances and one waltz for two unlikely souls to become hopelessly entwined. Mattie is determined to win the heart of this handsome, rugged man. Harry is just as determined to keep her safe.

Will fate find a way to bring a common man and an earl's sister a happy ever after? Or will his lack of title and dangerous life keep her at arm's length?

**Pads, Purses, and Plum Pudding #2**

Dr. Sampson Brooks is on a case that has nothing to do with medicine. He vows to help bring down the man who ruined his father and sent his mother to an early grave. When the villain's top henchmen are apprehended, Sam attends the hanging. While closing one chapter of his story, he unexpectedly opens another.

Dottie Brown, young and naïve, is duped by a charming swindler. A year after the wedding, she learns he's not what he pretends to be. Watching him on the gallows, she vows never to be taken in by romantic notions again. Yet fate tosses two obstacles in her path that day—a handsome physician and an abandoned child.

A chance encounter reveals one woman's secret, another man's revenge, and a love that will change their lives forever.

**Poisons, Potions, and Parasols #3**

*She's content with her life...*

Miss Eugenia Chapelle was born on the wrong side of the blanket. After her mother was disowned and fled to London, she pretended to be the widow of a French aristocrat to draw customers as a modiste. After her mother's death, Genie continues the lie, playing the half-French designer of Madame Chapelle's and running the business with her aunt. She never expects an earl to search out his illegitimate daughter twenty-six years later.

*He will rip it apart...*

Mr. Clayton Pierce works for one of London's most respected investigators. He has two cases on his docket—tracking a gang of counterfeiters passing banknotes and finding a long-lost child of an earl. When he meets the beautiful and talented Miss Chapelle, his attraction for her is as strong as his obsession with solving mysteries and catching criminals.

After Genie witnesses a possible murder at Hyde Park, she becomes a key witness in his first case. Then, by a twist of fate, she also becomes linked to his second assignment. With danger lurking around every dark corner, and the past the murkiest shadow of all, Clayton learns that solving a case does not always guarantee satisfaction of a job well done. As passions flare and the stakes are raised, will his success as an investigator be his ruin in love?

**Rogues, Rotters, and Rubies #4**

*A fiery-haired beauty...*

Clara Alberts, known affectionately as Ruby to her family and friends, has worked hard to craft her skills as a cook. When a French count moves into the influential Hatton Garden, she gets the chance to display her talent and move up in the domestic world of the ton. Add a chance encounter with a handsome young Bow Street Runner, and Ruby decides fate is finally smiling down on her.

*A perplexing series of thefts...*

Elijah Norton is finishing his second year as a Runner when he's asked to look into some recent thefts in Hatton Garden. Each jeweler questioned has found only one set of jewelry stolen and cannot say how long it has been missing. As Eli searches for answers, he meets the beautiful Clara Alberts. She steals his heart at first glance, a true diamond in the rough.

*Justice or love...*

As the Peelers continue to search for more clues to the elusive Vicar and his vast criminal network, Eli discovers Ruby's father is linked to the anonymous villain. If he pursues the lead and questions Mr. Alberts, he'll lose the girl. Yet ignoring the information may put the Crown in peril. Will the truth bring clarity to their relationship or create an imperfection in their gem of an affair?

*Set in the hectic district of Cheapside during the Regency, Paddy's Peelers search the dregs of London with skill and cunning to bring criminals to justice and, perhaps, unexpectedly find love along the way. A sweet but action-packed romance.*

**Wakings, Wooings, and Wrongdoings #5**

Miss Kitty Felton is the bubbly cup of tea one looks forward to in the morning. She sees a ray of sunshine in any calamity. Working as a knocker-upper, she heads out as her father comes home from his job as a nightwatchman. Her newest client is a handsome man, though she's only seen his head as he waves from the window to show he has risen. She's a silly romantic who dreams of Mr. Cooper falling in love with her.

Mr. Benjamin Cooper is a solicitor. Raised by Paddy O'Brien

and his wife, his role in the family investigative service is to provide legal advice and help to bring cases to court. Ben hires a new knocker-upper to wake him six days a week. For the past week, he's only seen the top of her bonnet and the palm of her hand when she waves and bids him good day. When he finally sees her smiling face, he's shocked she's not old like the last one. Instead, he finds himself waking before Miss Felton arrives, so they can chat a bit before she moves on.

After a brutal murder in Cheapside, Kitty realizes she may have seen the villain escaping. Her father insists she stay quiet, but her conscience is telling her differently. She believes her new beau, Mr. Cooper, could be trusted with her secret without going to the constable.

Kitty confides in Ben, and he realizes the only way to obtain justice is with Kitty's testimony. Benjamin is torn between loyalty to the O'Brien's and his growing love for Miss Felton. Will his duty as a solicitor for Paddy's Peelers put the enchanting Kitty at risk and destroy their new and still fragile romance?

**A MacNaughton Castle Romance series**

**Highland Regencies**

"Witty and sensual!"

Verified Purchase Review

"Lovely characters and complicated family conflicts. You will easily get caught up in their lives."

Goodreads Review

**A Merry MacNaughton Mishap** (Prequel)

**Rone finalist, InD'tale Magazine, N.N. Light Book Heaven finalist**

Two feuding clans, one accidental encounter, a wee bit of holiday enchantment...

When Calum MacNaughton rescues a rival clan member from an icy drowning, he is unexpectedly rewarded with the clansman's most precious possession. Now Calum has until Twelfth Night to convince her to stay.

**Deception and Desire #1**

**Nominated for Rone award, InD'tale Magazine, N.N. Light Book Heaven award winner**

Two rebellious souls... An innocent deception... One scorching catastrophe...

Fenella Franklin's talents lie in numbers and a keen business mind, not in the art of flirtation. Lachlan MacNaughton has neither the temperament nor the patience to be the next MacNaughton chief, preferring to knock heads together rather than placate bickering clansmen. Their attraction sparks a passion they cannot deny. But will an innocent deception test their newfound love?

**Allusive Love #2**

A woman in love... An infuriating Scot... A tantalizing chase.

Kirstine has loved Brodie MacNaughton forever, but he considers Kirsty his best friend. When he turns to her for advice, she surprises him with an unexpected kiss that sends fire through his veins. When pride, Highland politics, and tragedy collide, he realizes how precious and allusive true love can be.

**A Bonny Pretender #3**

She's pretending to be someone she's not... His entire life is based on a lie...

Brigid MacNaughton becomes the perfect lady to placate her

family, then falls in love with a quiet, self-possessed Englishman. Lord Raines is smitten with the beguiling and demure Scot. If he divulges his scandalous parentage, will she still fall willingly into his arms? Bonny pretender vs handsome imposter… Can love overcome a double deception?

www.ingramcontent.com/pod-product-compliance
Lightning Source LLC
La Vergne TN
LVHW090951080826
845145LV00003B/970

* 9 7 8 1 9 4 6 5 6 0 4 6 9 *